D1525400

CAPTAIN
OF
HEARTS

CAPTAIN
OF
HEARTS

•

Jean Ann Moynahan

AVALON BOOKS
NEW YORK

Published by Thomas Bouregy & Co., Inc.
401 Lafayette Street, New York, NY 10003

PRINTED IN THE UNITED STATES OF AMERICA
ON ACID-FREE PAPER
BY HADDON CRAFTSMEN, BLOOMSBURG,
PENNSYLVANIA

To my dearest Tim, with gratitude for love, loyalty, and support, and with thanks to God, from whom all blessings flow.

Chapter One

As the taxi sped down the street, scattering the late-September leaves like timid flocks of red and gold birds, Deirdre wondered if she had been duped by those travel office posters of sunlit Bavarian streets and romantic green forests reminiscent of fairy tales and grand operas. She was tired, cold, hungry, and at this particular moment, sadly disillusioned with her notion that a year teaching in "foreign parts" would be the adventure of a lifetime.

She was standing in front of a bleak post, or kaserne, secured by a gray chain-link fence. Beyond this was a prospect of old gray buildings, predictably squared, spaced, and arranged like a military version of a planned community. She glanced across the street at what looked like a large grove of trees. As she thought how little the trees looked like a forest from which a shining knight might appear, a voice intruded on her musings.

"Excuse me, ma'am. This is a military post with restricted access for civilians. Do you have an appointment with someone on post?" the earnest, fresh-scrubbed (or was that just the chill autumn air?) young soldier asked.

"Actually, I'm the new instructor for the university extension classes." Full stop. No reaction. Deirdre continued, "That is, yes, in fact, I do have an appointment with a Captain Mackenzie." Ah, that elicited a reactive change in expression. The young soldier visibly straightened, impressed.

"Yes, ma'am! Sorry, ma'am. I didn't realize the CO was expecting you. Just a moment and I'll call company HQ." He ducked into the guardhouse and made a call. A moment later, the head popped through the guard window. "The captain is sending his driver right over, ma'am."

Why did he have to keep calling her "ma'am"? She was, after all, only thirty—and only just. A rather young-looking thirty, thought Deirdre defensively. A still single thirty. The breakup with her fiancé was still tender territory and no doubt one of the reasons why a year in Germany seemed a good idea, a year to transition to a new life without Mark, who was a good long-term boyfriend but turned out to be a lousy short-term fiancé.

She was shaken out of her brief, melancholy reverie by the sound of tires crunching on gravel. A dark olive military sedan drove up alongside the guardhouse. Deirdre muttered a quick thanks to the guard and jumped in before the driver could get out to open the door. The car was pleasantly warm after even a few moments in the chill breeze of a fall morning.

"Hello there!" The resonant, deep-timbred voice had an oddly soothing effect on her frayed nerves. The captain certainly had a great welcoming committee. The driver's appealing voice was complemented by his unusual amber eyes that twinkled like fool's gold, and dark auburn hair, fairly close-cropped but betraying a slight waviness. His fair complexion wore the healthy flush of one used to being outdoors.

As she settled into the seat, grateful to be at least at the end of her journey—the early morning train ride from Frankfurt had been tiring—Deirdre attempted to acknowledge the greeting and introduce herself at the same time. "Hi, thanks for the lift. I'm Deirdre Lonagan, the new—"

"The new tutor. Yes, I know."

"Tutor? Well, I'm the *instructor* for the university credit classes that are to be offered on post for the coming academic year." It was a sore spot with Deirdre that someone who had spent so many years of study gaining a graduate degree should be dismissed so lightly as a "tutor." A clerk at the extension office in Frankfurt had made the same mistake.

"Instructor? Oh, sure, sorry." Pause. "Frankly, I think a tutor would have been a better idea. I'm just not sure that on-base full-credit classes are going to work." The driver spoke with nonchalant confidence, which annoyed Deirdre as much as the presumption of his remark.

"I beg your pardon?" She had been at her new, exciting, chance-of-a-lifetime job a matter of moments, and she was already getting her Irish up. She had been warned by her supervisor that there might be some resistance to the college classes. To be sure, the military brass responsible had already given their collective blessing to the idea, but translating that into grassroots support was something else. In fact,

Deirdre had learned through the university extension office in Frankfurt that Capt. Mackenzie had been vociferous in his displeasure at having the classes offered on his post. Clearly, the attitude had rubbed off on his driver, who suddenly didn't seem so appealing.

The driver cocked his head slightly, smiling at her with both his eyes and his mouth. "I just meant that the demands of a military mission will *always* come before Shakespearean sonnets and expository essays." Again, that smile that seemed to express amusement, affection, and just a hint of superiority all at once. He was starting to seem awfully appealing again.

Deirdre was also beginning to think that this driver—corporal, private, sergeant, whatever— was rather cheeky when she noticed the black two-bar insignia on his olive-green fatigue collar. *Oh. The man himself. Captain Mackenzie.*

"Are you Capt. Mackenzie?" Deirdre was both intimidated and embarrassed that she hadn't realized it before.

He grinned. "Yes. I apologize. I should have introduced myself immediately, but . . ." He smartly turned the car into a tiny parking spot next to a small, dingy building that sported areas of peeling plaster. "But I was so interested in finding out about *you* that my manners slipped." Now he wasn't just smiling, he was practically laughing. But it was a nice, mellow good-natured laughing, as if he found everything slightly amusing.

Before Deirdre could even respond, the handsome, smiling Capt. Mackenzie had jumped out of his side of the car as if he were parachuting at 15,000 feet and was swinging her door open, letting in an abrupt reminder of the rather damp coolness of the late morning.

"Come on, Ms. Lonagan. Let's get inside. There's always plenty of coffee around here. Normally I wouldn't vouch for the quality except that this morning *I* made it—so it's *great.* It's also very, very hot." His arm unexpectedly and firmly grasped her hand to help her out of the car, an almost courtly gesture that surprised her. Also, though it may have just been the warmth of a human hand, Deirdre seemed to feel a fluttery sensation as the captain escorted her into company HQ. But then, this was supposed to be the adventure of a lifetime, she thought wryly.

If not exactly fluttery excitement, Jack Mackenzie, Capt. U.S. Army, felt unaccountably off balance by this slender, intense young woman. Surely the black hair, porcelain skin, and hazel-green eyes flashing with intelligence and curiosity spoke of an Irish heritage. Beauty *and* temperament. An irresistible combination, at least according to his flamboyant and very Irish grandmother. The corners of his mouth creased slightly in a private smile as he thought of his Gran Mackenzie. Molly *Reilly* Mackenzie. She had been not unlike Deirdre in looks. Equally, she was smart, independent, high-spirited—and tough enough to withstand with grave dignity the loss of two sons to war and an adored husband to cancer. Jack had idolized her. Beauty and temperament.

He was especially vulnerable in this particular time and place. It wasn't that there weren't women on post, but virtually without exception they were enlisted women or fellow officers' wives, both strictly off limits. He had occasionally allowed his friends, both American and German, to play matchmaker with some of their attractive single women acquaintance, but it had been a while since he had had even one of those rather sparkless social evenings.

It was so easy to throw himself into his work. A lot of time and effort had been invested in his life to this point. West Point. Assignments in less-than-desirable locales around the world. And, of course, the ever-present objections of the Mackenzie clan, such as it was, who protested that Mackenzie Wood Industries needed him more than "this man's army." But as much as he loved his family and their business and traditions, he didn't want to spend his life riding herd on the already-built fortune of timber barons. Or at least that had been his feeling until recently. At any rate, he thought, whenever he missed those rainy Oregon fall days—*or* winter days *or* spring days—he had only to look out the window: southwestern Germany wasn't much different.

But now he had a new situation to deal with. He had misgivings about allowing enlisted personnel to take regular college credit classes while serving in a tactical signal company. This distractingly attractive young woman who now personified that problem didn't make it easier—for a number of reasons.

As the captain seemed to suddenly become silently preoccupied with fixing a tray of coffee and pastry, Deirdre looked about the office into which she had been ushered. Several enlisted men and women seemed efficiently and briskly attending to a variety of paperwork duties in the outer office (where the much-anticipated hot coffee was being prepared by the captain).

The captain's personal inner office was largely what she expected: all the accoutrements and insignia of an officer were present. But there was something more. She noted a few knick-knacks and desk items that had an "old money" feel—not exactly government issue. Although there were several family-reunion–type photos propped on his desk and on a nearby lawyer's bookcase, she couldn't help but notice there were no pictures of a wife or children. Not an infallible sign, but surely a military man used to long separations would have such evidence of a domestic history if one existed. Deirdre then realized the drift of her thoughts, and felt like giving herself a reality slap: this was hardly the time or place (or person, for that matter) to start daydreaming about.

"Here we are. As promised, coffee hot and masterfully made! I've added some pastry from the local bakery. Wonderful stuff, especially for those not on a diet." Instinctively his eyes wandered down the length of her slight but shapely figure before he caught himself. He cleared his voice and continued. "Well, anyway, it beats mess hall desserts by a mile, or as we like to say in this neck of the woods, a kilometer." He deftly placed the tray on the desk, then sat in the black leather chair opposite Deirdre.

As she poured cream into the steaming coffee mug, Deirdre couldn't help but notice that without his fatigue cap, Capt. Mackenzie looked younger than she had first thought; he was perhaps in his early thirties. His face still had an attractive chill-induced redness about his cheeks; his eyes, with their striking deep-golden hue, somehow seemed to sparkle more because of it. She felt more uncomfortable and awkward than she had expected to, but she was also enjoying it.

Capt. Mackenzie sipped his black coffee, observing the graceful movement of Deirdre's hands among the coffee things. "Ms. Lonagan, I don't want to offend you, and I believe I did earlier. I have read your file—yes, even civilians have a file if they work for Uncle Sam—and I realize you're an accomplished academic. A Ph.D. at twenty-nine, six years as a teaching assistant at a prestigious university, *and* a published dissertation. I was impressed before I met you." He paused. "And nothing has transpired in the last fifteen minutes to lessen my admiration for your, uh, achievements. But frankly I'm a little mystified. Why exactly do you want to spend a year at a job for which you are clearly overqualified?" He was impressed with Ms. Lonagan in more ways than one.

Although the warm office, pleasantly evocative of leather and a very faint citrusy aftershave, and the creamy hot coffee and walnut pastry were doing a lot to both restore her energy and soothe her slightly jangled nerves, Deirdre was still on edge. She regarded the captain's question as arrogant and patronizing. "Capt. Mackenzie, I'm not here to interview for a position. I already *have* the job, whether you're happy with that or not. This was intended as a courtesy call, but allow me to remind you that I do *not* need your permission to conduct classes for the University. That has already been granted by your superiors." Deirdre put a slight emphasis on the last word. She hoped that she didn't sound as shrill as she feared, but she resented the dashing captain's self-confidence and self-assurance.

As Capt. Mackenzie continued to gaze at her steadily, almost as if she were a butterfly specimen pinned to a slide, Deirdre continued. "I don't quite understand your opposition to the classes, Captain, but I am eager to devote myself to this . . . this endeavor because I believe everyone deserves the chance to get the best education he or she can—even those serving in the military. *Especially* those serving in the military."

What she didn't feel like revealing, what she wasn't sure was in her file—and how did those files get compiled, anyway?—was that she herself came from a military family, except that her father wasn't an officer. He was the son of Irish immigrants, of a time and generation when a lifetime in a police force or a fire department was an honorable achievement for someone whose grandparents had still spoken Gaelic in a poor, remote village in Donegal. Instead of the local police or fire department, her father had joined the army. He was a career enlisted man who worked hard for his family and his country, and whose life was cut short by a car accident at the age of forty-two while he was on his way to a night class in history. She had gone to that "prestigious" university on full scholarship, the result mostly of hard work and ambition, and maybe a bit of the "luck of the Irish." But that was ironic, wasn't it? Deirdre remembered that it really meant no luck at all, which summed up her current feeling fairly well.

There was a long pause; the murmur of busy clerks in the outer office intruded on the awkward silence. Deirdre thought for a moment that the captain was going to throw her out. At this point, she didn't much care. His calm, detached, amused manner was appealing, intimidating, and infuriating all at the same time. When he finally spoke it was very softly.

"Ms. Lonagan, I again apologize if I ruffled your feathers. But the fact remains that this is a military post, and I am company commander of a tactical signal unit that has to, with some frequency, go on field shots, participate in war games, pull twelve-hour radio shifts, etc. etc. etc. This is *not* a college campus. While I'm all for my troops furthering themselves, the traditional method to do that has been through correspondence courses. Such courses do not interfere with the day-to-day operations of the military."

"Correspondence courses do not give students, especially in writing and literature, the feedback they need," Deirdre rejoined heatedly.

"*I* give them the feedback they need!" The cool, calm captain was beginning to add his own heat to the discussion. Continuing in a slightly louder voice, he added, "Besides, I really don't see why a cryptic teletype operator needs to waste time analyzing dreamy poetry and expressing himself in sensitive journal writing." This last was said with a gesturing that seemed to say, "top that if you can!"

A thought occurred to Deirdre. "Correct me if I'm wrong, Captain, but you're not the only CO on this post, are you?"

Capt. Mackenzie seemed taken aback. "Well, no. There are three signal companies on this post, but as we are temporarily without an assigned battalion commander on post, I am also acting battalion CO."

"Does that mean you make the other COs parrot your opinions?" She couldn't resist the deliberate taunt and was secretly amused that it hit home.

"Ms. Lonagan, I think you have a lot to learn about the military," he answered through clenched teeth.

Deirdre, no stranger to the vagaries of moods and temper, was nonetheless momentarily taken aback by the controlled fury in the captain's voice. Clearly she wasn't the only one whose feathers could get ruffled. Strangely, the intensity of his annoyance made him even more attractive than the quiet polish of his officer-and-gentleman role. Before she found herself even more unnerved by the deepening realization that the captain was a very attractive man, Deirdre decided to take her leave gracefully.

"Captain, thank you for the coffee. I'm sure I will be seeing you in the future. My supervisor at the University has already advised me of which building I am to use for my classes, so your further kind assistance will not be needed. Good-bye." She rose from her chair and walked quickly from the room, silently thanking her lucky stars that she didn't mar such a grand exit by tripping on the unraveled threshold carpet.

A fuming Capt. Mackenzie stared after her. "Right. See you around the quad, Ms. Lonagan." What bothered him more than anything was not the apparent failure to halt what he considered civilian ivory-tower interference, but that the interference was so charmingly packaged.

While he listened to Deirdre Lonagan's footsteps fade through the outer office and then through the weather-buffering anteroom, their quickness eloquently expressing an angry passion, Capt. Mackenzie realized he was looking at a cedar-framed photo of the Mackenzie clan on his desk. And the smiling, pixielike face that caught his eye in particular was Molly O'Reilly Mackenzie.

Chapter Two

Deirdre felt her cheeks burning as she walked out of the company HQ. What a maddening man!

"Hey, there, careful." Deirdre looked up into the grinning round face of a blond, blue-eyed giant. "You look a little lost. Can I be of service?" he asked with a dazzling smile and a slight mock bow.

"I'm sorry. I guess I should look where I'm going."

"No problem. By the way, I'm Lieutenant Phillips—Lane Phillips. I'm the XO." Noting her puzzled expression, he added, "The executive officer, second in command to Capt. Mackenzie."

Deirdre nodded; of course, her supervisor had mentioned him. Mrs. Knight, the supervisor, had indicated that the lieutenant at least was on her side and had been helpful in handling the logistics of space, equipment, and supplies. He at any rate thought that adult education classes were a great idea.

"I'm happy to meet you, Lt. Phillips. I'm Deirdre Lonagan, the instructor from the University."

"I thought so! And call me Lane. I'll bet you haven't been to your accommodations yet, have you? Let me walk you over. It's not far. I can point out some of the scenic wonders of the place along the way: the snack bar, the laundromat, the NCO club, etc." He laughed— not as intriguing as the complicated Capt. Mackenzie, perhaps, but Deirdre immediately felt comfortable and at ease with the lieutenant.

"I would appreciate that, Lane. And it's Deirdre."

"Great. Let's go, Deirdre."

They walked down several narrow, graveled streets where Deirdre saw plain, squat office buildings of two or three stories fronted by modest strips of grass and ringed by low-hung chains and wooden posts, as if to keep these passive gray monsters of architecture from escaping their paddocks. Finally they arrived at what looked like a sturdy old gray prison. So much for romance and high adventure in the fabled Teutonic countryside. As they opened the door and entered a small reception area, a young woman rose from a metal desk, saluted, and walked toward them.

"Good afternoon, sir. Ma'am." She was an attractive redhead, mid-twenties, with a sprinkling of freckles on an almost childlike face.

"Good afternoon, Specialist Shubert." Did Deirdre imagine it, or for just a moment longer than necessary did the enlisted woman and the tall lieutenant look into each other's eyes? "Uh," Lane sputtered slightly, "Deirdre Lonagan, this is Specialist Shubert. She is the senior enlisted woman in this barracks and will be your roommate, at least until the first of the year." Lane paused, and again a look passed between the two that spoke of something in common beyond daily inspection in the company's yard.

"I'm pleased to meet you, ma'am. I've been expecting you. Let me show you to your—our—room." She looked around Deirdre, as if there must be a duffle bag or steamer trunk hiding. "Do you have any gear?"

"My supervisor, Mrs. Knight, is arranging to have it sent tomorrow. I have everything I need for tonight in my bag," Deirdre answered, giving a tug on the deceptively capacious leather and canvas purse-cum-carryall that fit over her shoulder.

Spec. Shubert smiled. "Right. Well." She glanced at Lane, who nodded.

"I can see that you have everything in hand, Ann—I mean, Shubert. You'll be fine, Deirdre. Until later." He then turned and strode out the door.

Deirdre and Spec. Shubert stood for a moment looking after his towering figure as it disappeared around the corner of yellow-washed brick office building.

"How *tall* is he?" Deirdre asked, shaking her head in amused disbelief.

Shubert turned, her face lit up with a grin. "Six foot five and a half." The exactness of the answer betrayed a more than passing interest in the XO. Deirdre smiled knowingly. No wonder the lieutenant had been so eager to escort her to her new digs. "Well, let's see that room of ours."

*   *   *

The barracks seemed relatively small. The downstairs comprised a common area with television, pop machine, guard desk, and judging by a quick glance down the hall to where a door stood open, several small rooms similar to those found in a dorm. To her far left, in what was presumably a common bathroom, Deirdre could hear a shower running. Otherwise, everything was very quiet.

Noting Deirdre's cursory inspection, Spec. Shubert offered helpfully, "There are six rooms downstairs, eight up, most with double occupancy." She nodded toward the shower and bathroom area. "One common area for personal ablutions. Most of us have nine-to-five shifts, more or less, most of the time. Of course, during field shots, shifts change, and there is always at least one person who has pulled a twelve-hour radio or guard shift, so you'll hear someone taking a shower at odd times. Like now. Come on, let's go up."

As they started bounding up the stairs like schoolgirls, Deirdre asked, "By the way, what is a 'field shot'?"

Spec. Shubert continued skipping up the stairs. "Oh, it just means a maneuver in the field, you know, overnight. Many overnights, sometimes."

They had arrived at the second floor, which was almost an exact replica of the bottom floor except two extra rooms took the space of the common area below. "We're at the end." Shubert waved Deirdre ahead of her.

The hallway did remind her of a college dorm. She had always felt lucky that she had been able to have her own apartment, albeit small, when she went to school. She wasn't too keen on sharing quarters with so many others; she liked her privacy and quiet moments. Still, it was bound to be an experience.

Shubert unlocked the flimsy-looking door and stepped aside proudly. "Here we are!"

Deirdre was immediately struck by how neat and orderly everything appeared. No doubt that was partly military discipline but she noticed the small vase of fresh flowers on the sill of the sparkling clean windows, the colorful hearth rugs that had been place next to the twin metal beds, one on either side of the room. She was touched by the obvious care, anticipation and pride with which her roommate had prepared for her arrival.

"It's perfect, Spec. Shubert."

Shubert beamed. "Good. I hope you'll be comfortable. And it's Ann, for Pete's sake."

"Deirdre. I hope I'm not putting you out by being a forced guest like this."

"Oh, no. It *is* a perk to have a room to yourself, but frankly I miss having someone to talk to, borrow a sweater from, you know. It'll be fun to have company. Besides, I won't be here after the first year. I'm a short-timer." Again, that grin that made her young-looking face seem even more youthful. "Hey, it's after noon. How about lunch? Unload anything you want to"—she motioned to a small nightstand by the bed on the left side of the room—"and we'll go down to the snack bar."

The snack bar at lunchtime was crowded with enlisted men and women talking and laughing as they ordered cheeseburgers, chili dogs, french fries, chicken salad, brownies, coffee, Cokes. The scene made Deirdre think of a cross between an old-fashioned high school malt shop and a singles bar. She and Ann made their way to a corner table after buying the most popular fare: cheeseburgers and Cokes.

"The food is simple but pretty good and reasonably cheap," Ann observed as she carefully removed the grilled onions from her burger.

"Isn't there a mess hall?"

Ann chuckled as she held the burger midway to her mouth. "And 'mess' is the operative word. No, it's not really that bad; they do a pretty good breakfast. But even though it's free to enlisted personnel, a lot of people prefer to come here. Partly for the food, partly because it offers a break from the military, sort of."

"I notice the officers aren't in attendance."

Deirdre was hungrier than she had realized and was hoping to keep Ann talking while she enjoyed the hot if somewhat greasy food.

"Sometimes they stop by, but there is a pretty clear dividing line between officer and enlisted."

"That seems rather antiquated—almost as if it's a division between aristocrats and peasants."

Ann frowned slightly. "Well, I wouldn't go as far as that. After all, everyone is here through voluntary commitment to service. And theoretically anyone can become an officer. Of course, there are educational requirements, among other things."

"So is it really true that there is no, what is the word, 'fraternizing' between officers and enlisted?"

Ann's fair redhead's skin blushed. "Well, yes, uh . . . that's true." Deirdre was sorry that she had embarrassed her new friend and room-mate, but she didn't see the point in being coy. "It's the lieutenant, isn't it?"

Ann nodded almost imperceptibly. "But for Pete's sake, don't let on. We have been so careful. You don't know how hard it is to see someone when it has to be a deep dark secret."

Deirdre felt a sting of envy for Ann and her furtive but no doubt exciting romance that obviously gave meaning to her life. She felt that stab of old pain, remembering when she and Mark had first started their relationship, how exciting it was just to know that she was going to see him for coffee or to discuss a book they had just read. Those waves of pain and memories came less frequently now, but they still sneaked up on her. Ann didn't know how lucky she was.

Ann had, in fact, continued talking, unaware of Deirdre's short failure of attention. "The worst was when Sgt. Cramer saw us at the Inn in town. *That* was hard to explain!"

"What do you mean?"

"The Inn is a nice—very nice—restaurant popular with wealthy locals. I forget the German name; we just call it the Inn. It's too expensive for enlisted, even most officers. I have no idea what Cramer was doing there. It was a special evening for us." Ann looked down at her left hand with a soft smile.

"Who is this Cramer fellow?"

Ann gave a short sharp laugh. "Not a fellow, a gal. The senior NCO—that is, noncommissioned officer—in the company. Very 'strack.' You know, by-the-book, starch-in-her-shirt kind of gal."

"Could you be discharged for being with Lane?"

"Oh, I don't know—they might transfer me. The worst damage would be to Lane. He's a career officer. Me, well . . ." She grinned from ear to ear. "I'll be out in December. I'm a two-digit midget!"

"A what?" Deirdre asked with a mouthful of ketchup-smeared fries.

"Two-digit midget. Means I have less than one hundred days to discharge. It's a milestone. We're going to be married before Christmas. As my official roommate, you're automatically invited; just don't breathe a word yet."

Deirdre caught the infectious joy of her friend and suddenly felt happy for two people she hardly knew. "Lane seems like a really nice guy." She paused, then tread carefully. "Capt. Mackenzie has his own appeal, too, I guess, but he does seem aloof as well. But I suppose his wife has learned to deal with that."

"Nice try, Deirdre. No, Capt. Mackenzie is *not* married—and I agree, he is incredibly good-looking, *if* I were looking, that is." Ann laughed, that sort of laugh that bubbles out of people like champagne when they are thoroughly happy. She seemed to have relaxed, too, since making Deirdre a confidante.

Now it was Deirdre's turn to blush. "I have to admit I did notice more than the bars on his collar." They both giggled. "He seems intelligent, too, in a complex way."

"Oh, definitely. West Point, top of his class. And of course, he's rich. Looks, brains, money—and he chose the Army! He really is a very decent CO, but he does have a certain social background that makes him seem—what is the word . . ."

"Patronizing?"

"Right. He doesn't mean to be and really isn't; it just sort of comes out that way sometimes."

Just at that moment, there was a lull in the noise level of the snack bar. Almost immediately the conversations began again if a bit more self-consciously. Capt. Mackenzie was making his way to Ann and Deirdre's table.

"Good afternoon, sir. I was just leaving." Ann smiled as she jumped out of her seat. She leaned down and whispered in Deirdre's ear, "There is *no* rule about officers fraternizing with *civilians!*"

The captain sat down. "I'm sorry if I interrupted your lunch. Why is it I always seem to be apologizing to you?" They both smiled, cleared their throats, and looked down at the table. "Uh, I really wanted to ask you to have dinner with me tonight." He had picked up an unopened packet of mustard from the lunch debris on the table and absently ran his finger over the serrated edge. "It's just, well, a peace offering, and we could make it a 'working dinner' too. We should talk a bit about the classes, schedule, and so on. How about it?" He seemed more unsure of himself than Deirdre would have thought possible from her encounter with him earlier.

Unsure or not, the gaze of those eyes, like sunburnt honey, unsteadied her. She only hoped that she was not blushing anew. His good looks and charm were even more disarming with this glimpse of vulnerability. She almost wished that he wasn't so likable. In fact, he was much more than likable. But she heard herself agree to dinner that night.

"Fantastic! I'll pick you up at six-thirty. I think I know the way to your place." He grinned. "There's a wonderful place in town, the Inn." She had to catch herself from acknowledging that she knew of it already.

She nodded. "Sounds good. See you at six-thirty then."

As Deirdre left the snack bar, Jack couldn't take his eyes off her. She had all the right attributes, but then a lot of women did. There was something else about this one, a light in her eyes when she was pleased (as he knew she was by seeing him just now), a fire—a green fire—in her eyes when she was passionate about something, as he had seen her this morning in this office. Maybe, maybe someday he'd see both at the same time: light and passion in the eyes of this lovely woman as she looked into his.

Suddenly, the captain came to from his romantic wool gathering (as his Gran Mackenzie would have put it), and realized that he had just asked a woman for a date in the snack bar of all places. He'd always regarded it as a particularly lively if grungy singles bar, minus the alcohol. Feeling both excited and a bit out of place, he walked to the door as some of his troops wondered what red-letter event had brought the CO in for a burger and Coke.

Chapter Three

As they drove the short distance to the Inn, Deirdre had to keep reminding herself that she had been on post less than twenty-four hours, yet here she was going out to dinner with a dashing stranger. Yes, she thought, that rather old-fashioned word fit the tall, aristocratically-featured captain. She was wearing an outfit borrowed from Ann, a green shot silk dress with a green-and-gold brocade jacket. Her own things were still en route from Frankfurt, but her plain black pumps were serviceable if not ideal for evening. She was fortunate that she and Ann were the same size, though Deirdre's extra height made the hemline a bit more daring than it probably was on Ann. She was a little surprised that the unfussy Ann had had such an outfit, but even women in the military had to have their extravagances, she supposed.

For his part, Jack looked every inch the gentleman with his casual but well-cut houndstooth jacket and tan slacks. He looked even more handsome than in uniform.

She felt the awkwardness of first-date jitters as the streets of Neuberg, alternately cobbled and paved, quaint and modern, rolled past. She kept telling herself this was *not* a date, but that didn't quell the excitement and the tension she felt sitting next to this powerfully built and for the moment silent captain.

"Captain Mackenzie, how long have you been assigned to this post?" *My, Deirdre, what a brilliant question.*

He smiled as he kept his eyes on the road. "Look, it's going to be a long evening if we maintain this sort of formality. I'm Jack."

Deirdre felt a little of the tension evaporate, though that electric sense of excitement remained. She laughed. "Okay, Jack. I'm Deirdre."

"Deirdre. Irish, of course. An unusual name, mythic almost. Deirdre." He repeated it softly as if it were a powerful chant. "It suits you." He pronounced his opinion as if she had been on the edge of her seat awaiting his approval. "What do people call you for short? DeeDee?"

Deirdre winced. "Not twice they don't."

He threw his head back and laughed. "Right."

She then realized that during this predictable but necessary get-acquainted banter, they had arrived at a restaurant that managed to look both "olde world" rustic and new-world elegant.

The interior continued this ambience. The aged oak paneling was warmed by ruby-red upholstered chairs and booths. Golden electric lights, several well-stocked fireplaces, and candle lamps on every table conveyed a cozy, romantic aura. The thick wool carpet with its fading scenes of bucolic lovers muffled the sounds of waiters and patrons. Deirdre felt famished as the smells of roast meats, spices, and sweet hot desserts floated around them.

Once seated, Deirdre stared at the oversized menus, silently cursing herself for taking four years of French instead of at least one year of German in college. She was afraid of making an utter fool of herself by ordering stuffed boar's head or ox-tongue soup with capers. However, Jack, with an impeccable sense of her predicament, spoke up.

"If you don't mind, I'd like to order my favorite for us both. I think you'll like it." His amber eyes looked both darker and more sparkling in the flickering fire and dim lights that played about the room.

Deirdre gratefully smiled her assent. "Sounds good to me whatever it is! Everything smells wonderful here!"

"Oh, it is." He then proceeded to order in what sounded like fluent German.

They nibbled at appetizers while waiting for the entrée, which turned out to be a delicious roast pork served with sweet peppers, shallots, a sherry sauce, and roasted vegetables on the side. She was so hungry that she lost her self-consciousness about talking and eating and managed to do both with alacrity.

After finishing coffee and a delicious apple-nut tart, they drank a soothing herbal liqueur that intensified the relaxing, almost hypnotic warmth and contentment that Deirdre felt after the wonderfully satisfying meal. Sleepiness, like summer gossamer, began to gently drift over her senses, but she resisted. She was glad of that week spent in Frankfurt with her supervisor; most of the "lag" in jet lag had been sloughed off. After the superficial conversation about adjusting to German customs, food, and transportation, Deirdre felt emboldened to ask Jack more about his background.

"Ann—that is, Spec. Shubert—tells me that you're from Oregon originally. Do you miss it?"

Jack shrugged, then smiled. "Well, I don't miss the rain because I only have to look out the window most the time. But seriously, yeah, I do miss it and my family. Spec. Shubert filled you in on my family's business?" This was said with an ironic raising of eyebrows.

Deirdre blushed, as she so easily did, her pale skin making it all the more obvious. The last thing she wanted was for Jack to think she already had spent her first afternoon on post gossiping about him—even if she had.

"Well, she did say that your family was in the timber industry. She didn't go into detail."

"No?" He chuckled softly. "It's all right, I don't mind talking about it. The Mackenzies— that is, my great-grandfather—made a fortune in timber around the turn of the century in the Mid-Willamette Valley of western Oregon. Although he had three sons, two were killed in World War Two, my grandfather being the surviving son. He also had three sons, but again war took its toll. Two of my uncles were killed in Vietnam. The only surviving son, my father, ran the business until he died two years ago. Lung cancer, just like his father. My mom had died several years before." He paused a moment and twirled a silver coffee spoon between his fingers. "Anyway, now it's down to my younger brother and me. We have distant maternal cousins who are involved in some aspects of the business, but it's really just the two of us—or now just him."

Again, he paused for a moment. For the first time he seemed genuinely melancholy, and for a moment had a faraway look in his dark golden eyes.

"Fortunately, Ron, my brother, enjoys the work. He finds it a challenge to develop new wood products, new harvesting methods, new approaches to conservation. He and his wife, Pat, travel a lot." Jack's face broke into an ear-to-ear grin. "And they have the cutest kid, a little girl. So, I guess the Mackenzie line will live on!" He made a mock toasting gesture and tossed back the last of the liqueur.

"So you've never been married before?" Deirdre hoped that she wasn't sounding too intrusive.

Again, a soft sadness came over his eyes like a bit of filmy cloud drifting across a late sun. He shrugged. "Once, but it was so long ago. It was a childhood sweetheart kind of thing. The romance really bloomed, in letters, when I went away to West Point. We were married at Christmas, and by the summer vacation we knew we'd made an awful mistake. It ended quietly and peacefully. She went on to be happily wed and careered, and I"—he shrugged— "didn't. It did show me that finding the right person isn't really about how long you've known each other. Maybe there really is some kind of mystical sixth sense that kicks in and tells us when Ms. Right, or Mr. Right, comes along. How about you? Been married?" Now he was playing with the lip of his crystal cordial glass, betraying an uneasiness at the personal nature of the conversation, perhaps, but also an interest in continuing it.

"Almost. I was engaged, until very recently. He was someone I met in grad school. We had a lot in common—in grad school. Like you, I discovered that someone who seemed perfect in one situation can look very different in another." Silence settled momentarily as if they were seeing the ghosts of other faces, other candlelit dinners, each in his own way.

Time for a change of subject. "Why did you choose the military? Not interested in the family business?" Deirdre was beginning to see that there was far more to Jack than she had thought.

"Oh, it's not that. I guess I just wanted to find my own way, meet my own challenges. Does that make sense?"

"Of course. I can understand that. It would have been easy for me to settle down to a lifetime in academy. I wanted something a little bit more—at least before I settle down."

Jack nodded slowly, looking at her with the same intensity that he had earlier in his office, but this time there was a compassion that had been lacking before.

As the hum of conversation around them gradually faded with the waning evening, Jack suggested they take a short walk. After the dinner and the warm, soporific air of the restaurant, the brisk, moist air that greeted them outside was welcome.

They walked slowly down the sidewalk, past cafés, taverns, bookstores, and small shops closed for the evening. Jack peered at her thoughtfully from time to time, cocking his head quizzically as if he were still trying to figure her out. "Why did you come here, to

Germany, so far from home? By the way, where is home?"

"Arizona. A beautiful place in many ways, but I got tired of desert and cacti and scorching sun. I'm not really sure yet where I want to settle; I didn't want to get on a tenure track at a university and then uproot myself after a year. At any rate, I thought a year in Europe would give me perspective. Well, I guess that brings us to a sore spot and the reason for this evening. And thanks for a wonderful dinner."

"You're welcome. And having dinner with you *was* a reason in itself." Deirdre felt a tremor of excitement at the thought that there might be more than a courtesy involved in his attentions. He was exasperatingly difficult to read. "But you're right. There is some business to discuss too."

They had to squeeze together briefly to let a loud and joyous group of students pass them on the narrow sidewalk. He smiled down at her for a moment, then continued. "Frankly, regular classes two or three times a week would not be feasible, not in a tactical signal unit."

"What is a tactical signal unit, anyway?" Deirdre tensed as she had earlier in his office, feeling that her whole reason for being in Germany was threatened.

"It simply means that we are in a constant state of readiness. We could be deployed anywhere in the world on twenty-four hours' notice."

"I still don't see how my classes would interfere. They meet once a week, three hours a class. One is basic expository composition and the other is a general survey of English literature—you know, Chaucer to Cheever. They are both excellent foundations for students who want to either continue at a community college or transfer to a regular four-year university."

"Deirdre," Jack said with quiet exasperation, "these are not students. They are military personnel in the U.S. Army, and they have duties and responsibilities. What the devil difference does it make whether they ever know who Chaucer was or how to interpret a Shakespearean sonnet?" His eyes had now lost the golden shine that had made them, and him, so handsome in the restaurant. His coppery hair looked darker, too, in the night air. Suddenly he seemed much more intimidating.

"And do *you* know who Chaucer was or how to analyze a Shakespearean sonnet?" Deirdre knew that her own eyes, set off by Ann's green silk, gleamed even more greenly when she was angry, which she was now.

"Of course I do! What do you take me for!"

"Exactly! This patrician versus peasant mentality the military fosters comes through loud and clear in you. You're an officer, so naturally you must be educated, but the lower orders, that's a different story."

"You don't know what you're talking about. Yeah, I know all that stuff that is supposed to make the well-educated man, but I'm not sure how much it affects my life on a practical, day-to-day basis. But I'm very, very sure that what I and my troops need to know to operate as a unit is very practical."

Silence fell between them like a slammed door, as if both recognized that they had let a lovely time between a man and a woman become a profound disagreement between two lifestyles, two philosophies. For some reason, this saddened and deflated Deirdre more than anything Jack had actually said.

Jack stopped in front of a darkened bakery and took a deep breath. "Look, I didn't mean for this to become a tit-for-tat debating match. Let's just drop it for now."

She silently assented, wondering with regret

if this good-looking, intelligent, and intense man would ever look past their obvious differences to the real Deirdre.

She had walked out of the restaurant carrying the brocade jacket, but the night was more than cool enough for it now. Jack helped her slip into it, his hands brushing her hair and bare neck as he did so, making Deirdre shiver slightly. As quickly as the squall had arisen, it departed, leaving her feeling again like an eighteen-year-old on a first date. "You look sensational this evening," Jack murmured. Deirdre whispered, "Thanks." And then they were back to being a man and a woman as swiftly as lightning tearing through a dark sky.

They drove back to the kaserne in comfortable silence, Deirdre wishing that the evening didn't have to end. She felt like Cinderella, and her Prince Charming still left her a bit intimidated, but feeling more alive than she had in a long time.

She knew that they must be very near the kaserne when Jack made a right turn into a forest park; in fact, she realized it was the grove of trees that lay directly across the street from the post's gates, but it was much, much deeper than she had thought. What light there had been from scattered street lamps and other cars' headlights vanished as the car slowly came to a stop amid the crunching of rock and snapping of small twigs.

"Do you like the forest?" Jack asked.

"Oh, I love forests. It's one reason why I'm sure that I don't want to go back to the desert. Forests have always seem the embodiments of so many things: fairy tales, desultory walks, permanence and change both." She stopped self-consciously as she felt his eyes on her. It was dark and she was looking straight ahead, but she felt those eyes all the same.

"I love them too. And not just because it's because it's the family business. They have an, what's the word, ineffable mystery, especially at night. I imagine how little they might have changed over thousands of years. Who knows, some primeval man—and woman—probably looked out on this very scene. It's just . . . I don't know, it's hard to put into words."

"Perhaps a Shakespearean sonnet could help you out." Deirdre hoped he could see her smiling in the dark.

"Touché, Deirdre." They sat for a moment, both lost in thoughts, hers sad and dreamy.

Then, almost on cue, as if they'd rehearsed this a thousand times, she turned to him and he leaned into her, his lips instantly finding hers with his. He gently stroked her hair as she felt lost in a timeless, fluid world, not dark but without light, comforting and unsettling at the same time. Then he abruptly pulled back and drew a deep sighing breath. "Oh, Deirdre. I don't know, I don't know . . ." He trailed off, muttering to himself as much as to her. "It's late. I'd better get you back."

She felt disappointed that the moment had passed, but also relieved: she wasn't sure how she should respond. Just as she had envied Ann earlier for her romantic intrigue with the friendly blond lieutenant, she now envied that primeval woman of so many generations ago for a simplicity, a lack of intrigue that she now yearned for.

He watched her slender form slip quietly into the barracks. Jack felt that a new complication had been dropped into his life. He had already begun to feel restless in his military career, felt the lack of stability, of family, of someone to come home to at night. Now this extraordinary woman—beautiful, intelligent, passionate—had walked into his life. And he wasn't sure if she was a signpost to a new life, or a reminder that his old one was still the right one.

Chapter Four

Deidre walked down the dim hallway of the quiet barracks. It was only just after 10:00 P.M., but the rooms were mostly silent. An occasional radio played softly, and she could hear that someone was taking a shower; otherwise, the roughly two dozen enlisted women who called this building home were already asleep. No doubt morning came early. Fortunately, Ann was still up; she looked up from the letter she was writing as Deirdre walked in.

"Have a good time?" she asked uncertainly.

"Okay, I guess. You were right. Jack is not as aloof as he seems at first. He was really quite the gentleman, and easy to talk to."

"But?"

"But nothing, really. It was a great evening." Deirdre thought a minute. She didn't readily confide in people but she could already sense that being in a foreign country forged friendships faster than normal.

Ann indicated the letter she was writing and asked, "Have any letters you need to write? Mom, Dad, boyfriend?"

Deirdre realized this was as good a way as any to open the subject. "Actually, I have, *had*, a fiancé. We broke up two months ago. I guess that's one reason why I took this job, to get away."

Ann nodded. "I wondered about that. I mean, you don't seem like the type to end up on a dumpy kaserne in Germany. Well, I guess you're not the first to want a change of scene to get over a broken heart. There's always the hope that the change of scene will bring a new chance at love and romance, right?" she asked, not unkindly.

Deirdre smiled weakly, deciding for a change of subject. "Is that what the lieutenant was, a change of scene?"

Ann laughed. "Oh, no, nothing like that. Our situation is more of a case of good friends realizing that there was more than friendly feelings involved. Unfortunately, we didn't realize that until *after* he became an officer."

Seeing Deirdre's puzzled look, Ann explained. "We met here last year when he was the sergeant of my platoon. He had put in months before for OTS—Officer Training School—then it finally came through. He was gone for six months and came back a second lieutenant. That six months' separation was the crunch time, I suppose. We wrote, chatty at first, then more and more personal. By the time he came back, we were in love—and separated by the Army's no-frat policy." Ann shrugged. "There's nothing we can do about it."

"I assume Jack doesn't know about you two."

"Heavens no! The CO is a good guy, but he is also very 'Army.' He and the lieutenant have a good working relationship, but he wouldn't hesitate to write up Lane if he realized we were involved. It's not a minor case of rule-breaking."

"It must be difficult."

"Yeah, it is. But it won't last forever." Ann's eternal optimism surfaced.

"Well, I guess I'd better let you turn in. I have a big day tomorrow, too: the first class meeting of the freshman composition class! I am scared silly that I'm going to walk into an empty room!"

"Don't worry about that. Lane and I have already signed up."

"Do you need the credits?"

"No, but we thought we'd give you some moral support."

"Many thanks. Two students guaranteed."

"Of course, I have to admit there was a self-ish reason also: it's a great chance for us to meet in the evening with a legitimate reason."

Deirdre smiled, glad for the morale-building whatever its ulterior motives. But she again felt a pang of envy for Ann's relationship, with its added zest of secrecy.

The fall day that had started sunny and mild had now turned chilly and windy. Although many trees still had much of their autumnal luxuriance, more and more leaves seemed to layer the narrow streets of the kaserne, sometimes hiding small puddles of the brief showers that punctuated the day. Some early casualties had already become slick brown smudges on the road and walkways, already disintegrating, slipping from the grasp of this season, awaiting their next reincarnation.

Deirdre had walked to a first meeting of a

class dozen of times during her years as a graduate assistant, but it never got any easier. The butterflies in her stomach fluttered as energetically as the falling leaves.

The kaserne was small and her walk to the building where her classes were to be held was short. As she found the room, she paused with her hand on the knob for a minute, took a deep breath, said a short prayer, and walked in.

What greeted her was a roomful of about twenty eager-looking faces. She quickly spotted Ann and Lane, who gave big smiles and waved. She walked to the lectern near a portable chalkboard. "Good evening. My name is Deirdre Lonagan." Her first class had begun.

An hour or so later her students were quietly writing their diagnostic essay so that Deirdre would have more of an idea of what their weaknesses and strengths might be. Deirdre sat absorbed in the textbook that had been ordered for the class. Suddenly, she was startled to hear a PFC near the door shout, "Att'n-*hut!*" Everyone rose with a scraping of chairs on the tile floor. Deirdre looked up to see Capt. Jack Mackenzie standing in the doorway looking as if he had just rounded up a nest of enemy spies.

Lane spoke first. "Good evening, sir."

Jack muttered a greeting. Then he looked at

Deirdre with a long searching gaze, hard to decipher. "I apologize, Ms. Lonagan, for the interruption, but I wanted to see how the class was going." *Or not,* thought Deirdre.

"It's going well, Captain, thank you for inquiring. As it is the first night, I was just about to let everyone off early." She turned back to face the class. "Please complete the reading assignment and journal entry we talked about earlier. And don't forget to hand in the writing sample essay on your way out. Good night— and thanks for coming!" This last was said pointedly while looking at Jack, who merely said, "Hmmm."

As the class filed out under the watchful eye of their CO, Deirdre tried to smile at each and take a mental snapshot of every face. She liked to get to know her students as people as well as academic achievers. Ann and Lane left first. Jack seemed to scrutinize them in particular. Then a few young women who didn't seem much different from her freshman students back home exited. These were followed by a couple of burly types who seemed awkward and out of place, but Deirdre admired whatever goal, educational or professional, that had brought them here tonight. The last one out was a young man with dark hair and eyes who had seemed the most attentive in class. He handed in what was clearly the longest essay of all, looking at her with an almost pleading yet excited glance as he placed it gently on the pile of papers.

Then it was just she and Jack. The classroom felt much bigger with only the two of them, yet somehow not big enough to hold all the emotion she sensed between them: tense, pleasing, disconcerting. It reminded her of their first meeting—had it only been the previous morning? Jack seemed ill at ease too. She thought he looked taller than she had remembered; perhaps the combat boots that were part of the uniform of the day added an inch or two to his six-foot frame. His deep-copper hair was slightly wind-tousled, giving him the appearance of a medieval warrior fresh from a skirmish. His eyes, like burned resin, were serious and inscrutable.

"I noticed your roommate is enrolled. *And* Lt. Phillips. Surely both already have at least a year of college. I know the lieutenant does."

Deirdre felt she had to cover convincingly for her friend. "They wanted to brush up on their grammar and style. And I suppose it was partly for moral support, too."

"Hmm. I guess. Though it doesn't look like

you need that." He waved his hand over the empty room as if dispensing a benediction. "Quite a turnout. Hope it's not going to be a problem."

As usual, Deirdre had managed to go from intimidation to exasperation with this man in very short order. "And why would it be a problem, Captain?"

Jack smiled. "Oh, so now it's 'Captain' again, is it? Look, I just don't want you to be disappointed if this doesn't work out."

"It *is* working out, don't you think?" Deirdre crossed her arms in a don't-even-think-about-disagreeing gesture.

Jack ran his hand through his hair, shaking his head slightly in impatience. "Let me walk you home; it's dark, and though this isn't exactly an urban crime center, there have been a few incidents."

Deirdre hesitated, but she was a little nervous about walking even the short distance back to the barracks. "All right. Maybe we could get some coffee or cocoa at the snack bar." She didn't relish the idea of a cold, fizzy pop back in her room.

"Sure. It's still open."

The snack bar was just, in fact, closing. They were still able to buy some hot apple cider—a hot water and mix, but it tasted good on this windy, chilly evening.

As they walked slowly back, each seeming to want to extend the time in each other's company without seeming obvious about it, Jack joked about the potential major prose stylists in her composition class.

Deirdre was still a little suspicious of what if anything Jack was going to do to thwart her classes. And her reason for being here. She bristled. "Just because they want to improve themselves doesn't mean they deserve to be patronized for their efforts."

Jack was amused. "Don't get your Irish . . ."

"Don't say it!" She hated it when people thought they understood her because of who her ancestors were, even if she sometimes tried to understand herself that way.

Jack held up his hands in a gesture of surrender, smiling all the time. "Okay, okay—don't . . . uh, allow your Celtic temperament to be piqued so easily." Deirdre bit her lip to keep from tossing fuel to the flame. "I hope, assuming the class continues, that my troops will benefit from it. After reading some of the logs and reports of my senior NCOs, I think they could all use a refresher course."

He was trying to keep peace over what was

clearly going to be bone of contention between them, but Deirdre was annoyed at the continued patrician attitude of this captain, who looked, she hated to admit, every inch the patrician.

"Maybe some of them have goals beyond writing logs and reports. Maybe some, will wonders never cease, actually intend to do something after or other than the Army. There *is* life outside this post or kaserne or whatever it is, you know. And by the way," Deirdre added, really having worked herself into a fine froth, "why are they *your* troops? You speak like a nineteenth century Russian landowner."

During most of her unloading, Jack had stood, looking at her with smoldering intensity. But her last remark changed his expression quickly.

"They are *my* troops because they are in *my* company under *my* command and *my* responsibility. Yes, Ms. Lonagan, I know there is life outside this post. But concentrating on the life *on* this post is one of the commitments—one of the sacrifices, if you will—that I made when I became an officer. A sacrifice that I'm still making, I might add. And your allusion to nineteenth century serfdom is absurd and insulting. You read too many novels, Ms. Lonagan. I guess an English degree is a good excuse for that."

They stood staring at each other, each regretting that their conversation had reached the level of anger and hurt pride yet again—but also finding that it seemed to concentrate the heat of the attraction between them like a magnifying glass in the sun.

Abruptly, without warning, Jack reached out with both hands and took her face into his, bringing his face so close that she could smell the sweet spice from the cider on his breath.

"Deirdre," he said softly, "why do you have to fight me?" He then bent down and kissed her gently at first, but then with a growing hunger. She responded slowly at first, but with a greater sense of being lost in the moment as autumnal breezes blew her hair, the long black waves whipping around his face and hands.

Just as abruptly as he had started, he stopped. He whispered into her ear, so close she felt the dampness of his breath. "You don't know everything about me, Deirdre, and you are being very unfair if you think I don't have needs and longings like anyone else."

He then stepped back, and without looking

at her again, directed her by the arm to the barracks door. Neither spoke as he left her at the door and walked back to the company headquarters.

Chapter Five

Deirdre spent the next day settling into her shared room. It was standard government issue, but Ann had made the most of it. Inexpensive but cheerful curtains of white-and-pink blown roses were pulled back with thick red yarn bows. Family photographs were scattered about a dresser, nightstand, and small bookcase. None of lane, of course. There was also an arrangement of dried everlasting flowers in a medieval-looking cobalt blue mug. Ann had made it clear that Deirdre could add whatever personal touches she wanted to—but what personal touches did she have to add? Deirdre felt both sad and frustrated to realize that she had nothing to contribute to even half of a barracks room. Before she got too drawn into pondering the possible symbolic meaning of that lack in her life, she decided to head to the PX on a nearby kaserne.

She took a taxi from the front gate, shaking her head in amazement again at the German use of Mercedes for taxis. The fifteen-minute ride to the neighboring post took her through some of the same streets she had been through with Jack two nights earlier. She could take in the sights more readily now, and noticed the small farms, rolling hills, and fields past their harvest. There were also reminders of a very modern, very technological Germany: expensive cars, exclusive shops, discreetly protected industrial parks.

The PX itself was like a huge American discount store, except that many of the goods were of exceptional quality: French perfume, Italian silk scarves, English china. It was a combination discount store *and* duty-free shop. She was grateful that one of the perks she enjoyed as a civilian employee was a PX card. She was also able to buy the usual personal items, feeling an unexpected comfort in being able to buy familiar name-brands from home.

Back in her room, she carefully unbagged

her various purchases. She placed a Wedgwood ring box on the nightstand. She smiled at the slight incongruity of having a ring box when she never wore rings. For some reason, she had always felt that the only ring she ever wanted to wear was a wedding ring, though at this point one didn't seem in the offing. She did, however, wear earrings virtually every day and an occasional pin on a scarf on a collar. It was a beautiful box, in any event. The blue-and-white jasper always reminded her of a favorite line from a Shakespeare sonnet: *"Rough winds do shake the darling buds of May."* White buds against a blue spring sky.

Next, she placed a handful of inexpensive cosmetics in the stand's drawer. These, she thought wryly, she would consider indispensable even if she were stranded on the moon. Finally, she took a small white handkerchief and folded in it her one truly extravagant purchase of the day: a small vial of Lancôme's "Magie Noire." She carefully tucked it in a corner of the drawer. Oh, well, a little vanity was good for the soul. And Deirdre instinctively knew that by such familiar signposts a woman kept her bearings in life.

Then she sat at the desk that she and Ann shared and began to read through last night's diagnostic essays. They were, for the most part, what she would have expected from any beginning writing class. Ann's and Lane's essays were good but had some commas, splices, and dangling modifiers she'd tease them about. The real surprise was an essay by an enlisted man, Juan Rodriguez, the young man with the bright, dark eyes. Although it was standard in many ways—explaining why he wanted to take the class, how he wanted to eventually become a lawyer on the GI Bill—the *way* in which he explained himself, used words, and conveyed a personality was most unusual and impressive. She smiled as she reread it, recalling one of her graduate professors speaking before a methods seminar of prospective teachers: *"Rarely will you encounter a student who writes beautifully, even better than you do. That is a joy, or should be."* It was.

It also reminded her of why she had come to Germany in the first place. Mark, the sometime boyfriend/fiancé, was only part of the reason, a secondary part. She really was committed to teaching, to making a difference. She would never believe that thinking well and writing well were dispensable niceties. And the most gratifying experience of all would be to help someone like Juan achieve his or her potential.

Lost in this pleasant if self-congratulating train of thought, she was startled by a quick rap on the door.

"Yes? Come in."

Again, a rap. Annoyed, Deirdre got up to open the door. There stood a veritable poster girl, or woman, for the U.S. Army. An NCO of about forty, with nondescript hair, Army-issued glasses, and cardboard-stiff fatigues stood glaring at her.

"Ms. Lonagan? This note was left on the desk for you." As she handed over a sheet of paper that had been folded in half and stapled, she peered over Deirdre's shoulder at the new additions to the room, including some inexpensive French Impressionist prints that Deirdre had picked up at the PX. "Are those pictures on *nails?*" Not waiting for an answer, she forged ahead. "*Any* proposed change in the structure of the walls should be submitted in writing to the barracks sergeant or CO— *FIRST. Should* permission be granted, an applicable form will be issued to the requesting party."

"I hardly think that a couple of nails in the wall qualify as a change in the—"

"Indeed they are a change," the NCO barked. "Small holes have been made in the wall; permission should have been sought and granted, as I have just indicated."

Deirdre looked at the offending prints and sighed in exasperation. "Look, I can take the pictures down if—"

"Rather too late for that, isn't it? The holes are there!"

"Then I guess there's nothing more to be said, is there?"

The woman stood squinting at the pictures a moment, reminding Deirdre vaguely of the wicked witch in the "Wizard of Oz." Finally, the NCO turned on her heel to walk away, and Deirdre noticed the green cloth name tag sewn on her fatigues: CRAMER. Of course. Deirdre could understand why Ann regarded her as a formidable enemy when it came to her secret engagement. She certainly did look like the kind of "strack" NCO who would turn in her own mother for an infraction of the rules.

Shaking her head, Deirdre closed the door and sat at the desk to open the note.

How about a day trip to Heidelberg? It is too late for the burning of the castle, but we could have dinner.

Jack.

The burning of the castle? What on earth was that—some obtuse romantic reference? She laughed out loud. She really did read too many books, perhaps. She decided to walk to the company HQ.

She was no sooner out the door of the barracks when she saw Jack walking with Lane on the narrow road in front of the building. Lane greeted her with a big grin, saluted Jack, and then turned back to the HQ.

"Got your note. I was coming to accept your invitation, though I am intrigued by the burning of the castle part. Gee, and I was so looking forward to it."

Jack grinned his pleasure at her acceptance. "Oh, that's a tourist thing they do in the summer. A few times a month, at dusk, they light up Heidelberg Castle with floodlights and set off firecrackers. It is spectacular to watch from the bridge across the Neckar River. It's impressive. But I'm afraid you'll have to be satisfied with a quiet supper with a picturesque view of the castle."

"That would be great. By the way, why did you have Sgt. Cramer bring me the note?"

"Cramer? Oh, I would have just as soon she not even know about it. I just gave it to the PFC on duty at the desk. Cramer is okay, but she would write up her dying grandmother if she thought it would further her own interests." Deirdre smiled as she realized their opinion about Cramer was in agreement, if nothing else.

He picked her up at 5:00 with twilight already descending. Her luggage from Frankfurt had arrived, thankfully, and she had been assured by Ann that slacks, a spun-silk turtleneck, and a fine-wale corduroy jacket would be suitable for an evening in Heidelberg. Deirdre was glad to see that Jack had dressed with the same studied but comfortable casualness.

As they drove out of the quaint, sleepy environs of Neuberg Kaserne, she noted that she was beginning to feel more relaxed in his presence. She also noted that the excitement that she had felt each time in his presence was no less intense—in fact, it was more so. She couldn't look at his face, his hands, his arms without thinking of the evening a few days earlier when he had kissed her so tenderly, yet almost with a sense of hopelessness. Why?

It was a lovely autumn evening; the trees unburdened themselves reluctantly of their burgundy and gold and copper leaves with each gust of wind. She again felt that peculiar excitement and longing that made her want to hold on to this moment indefinitely, to stay with Jack in this warm car which smelled slightly of leather, and ride on and on into the night.

"Have you been on the Autobahn much yet?" Jack also seemed more relaxed, but still felt the need apparently to make small talk.

"No, not really. I stayed with my supervisor in Frankfurt a week, then took the train to Neuberg. I have heard that it is an amazing freeway."

"That it is. Scary, perhaps, for some foreigners. But it gets you where you're going fast." He gave her a quick glance and a grin as he swung onto an exit ramp.

In a matter of minutes they could see Heidelberg spread out before them. Deirdre thought it looked the way anyone who had ever seen "The Student Prince" would imagine a small German university town.

The town was laid out on either side of the Neckar, a lazy, winding river that seemed to split the beautiful valley in two. The hills were thickly forested and as they drove further down she could see huge estates secluded behind ironwork fences. It was certainly picturesque. As they came to a stop in the main part of town, Deirdre felt she had stepped back through time via a painting.

"It's charming, isn't it?" Jack seemed eager that she should be impressed, which she was.

"Absolutely. Oh, I can see the castle now." It was perched like a great stone guardian above the town. "I can imagine it would be spectacular under floodlights and fireworks."

"Yes, it is," said Jack. "I'm sorry we can't see that, but after dinner we could drive up and walk around. The grounds are open, even some of the rooms."

Deirdre readily agreed. They started to wander through the rain-washed cobblestone streets. She saw many young people who were obviously either students at the University or the student and intellectual wanna-bes that such an ancient and romantic university was bound to attract. Many couples were strolling lazily, hand in hand. Suddenly, she realized that Jack had taken her hand, as if they too were a romantic young couple. Well, why not? She again felt as if Jack were holding something back, however. Even the hand-holding had a tentative feel, but she wanted to just enjoy the moment.

Ultimately, Jack stopped in front of a small restaurant whose heavy oak door, mullioned windows, and weather-worn stones looked as if they had seen countless generations of students come and go. They entered. A friendly blond waitress, no doubt a student, directed them to a comfortable leather booth next to a window with a lovely view of the castle.

Jack ordered, and they chatted inconsequentially through an agreeable dinner. Then, rather than linger over dessert and coffee, Jack suggested they visit the castle, as the grounds closed at 10:00 P.M., and they still had the hour or so drive back to the kaserne ahead of them.

Driving into the grounds of Heidelberg Castle was even more awe-inspiring than viewing it from across the river. Jack explained that it was one of the oldest, best-preserved castles in Europe. The moss-covered brown-and-gray stones of the huge building, hundreds of years old, made Deirdre feel somehow humble and insignificant. It was already dark, but some student society, probably the equivalent of a fraternity, was having a fancy-dress dinner in one of the banquet rooms, and the grounds were lit. The smell of candles and wood mingled. Only a few others were on the walkways. The gardens were denuded of most of their high summer color, and the light-absorbing dark green of fir, moss, and fern dominated the walls, benches, and trellises.

As if attuned to her thoughts, Jack said, "It makes you feel kind of small, doesn't it, all this history? Just think: this has been here for centuries, has seen war and peace, love and hate, babies coming into the world, old people going out." He looked over his shoulder as the student society festivities swelled to a momentary roar. He smiled. "Young people thinking, *knowing,* they have life fanning out before them, an unstoppable flood of adventure and possibilities . . ." He seemed to catch himself. Why did men always seem to be self-conscious about saying anything slightly thoughtful or introspective? "I didn't mean to sound morbid."

"You didn't. I was just thinking the same thing. You start to wonder what of yourself you'll leave behind. A lovely old place like this brings it to the surface. But, frankly, I would have thought that a career officer would have a sure sense of himself and his destiny."

Jack had been listening appreciatively to her agreement, but when she turned the conversation back on him, his life, he seemed to once again retreat.

He was thoughtful a moment, then said, "Don't stereotype me too much." He grinned.

"Don't you warn your literature students about that?" He shrugged and added, "Who knows, maybe I'm not cut out to be a career officer after all. Maybe I'm in the mood for a change of destiny."

Deirdre felt her part now was to be quiet and listen. Jack continued. "Ever since I was fifteen, I've wanted to be an officer. Maybe because my family, like so many others, has sacrificed through two devastating wars. I wanted to make my own contribution, but as an officer." They had come to a bench in a bend of the walkway. He said, "Let's sit for a minute." The stone was cold, the moss damp, but Deirdre didn't want to disrupt his train of thought, which was obviously an unburdening.

He continued. "It was a boyhood dream to go to West Point. It was a lot of work, but I have loved every minute of it. But I'm beginning to wonder if I might eventually regret the rootlessness of military life." He turned to look at Deirdre, reaching out and smoothing her hair, almost unconsciously. He then let his hand drop. "Who knows? Maybe I'm going through a phase"—he waved at the diminishing fall foliage—"a season. I'll probably regain my equilibrium by the next change of season." His wry smile indicated he was already sorry that he had spoken so personally, but Deirdre wasn't going to let it drop.

"People aren't trees, Jack. Sometimes changes occur and should. No one is locked into a destiny. Don't be afraid to face questions about, well, whatever makes you long for a different kind of stability."

"Do you ever feel like that? Do you want to settle down, have a family, claim one spot of earth as your own, and make your mark on it?"

Deirdre felt herself blushing slightly because that was exactly what she was thinking. And thinking that right now the only thing she really wanted was to claim that spot of earth and settle down with the man sitting next to her. "Yes," she responded simply. "Yes." She knew by the way he turned his body toward hers, by the way he let his arm gently circle her waist, that she didn't have to say anything more. He kissed her then, soft and long, and the mingled fragrance of the banquet fireplace, the damp woods, and his leather jacket made her think of a warm and cozy den in which they could shut out the rest of the world and be wrapped in each other's arms. But that time was not yet—if ever.

* * *

As they drove back to the kaserne through the dark, foggy night, Jack glanced down at the glossy dark hair of Deirdre's nestled head, feeling her warmth, smelling her lingering perfume. He smiled as he thought that they had reached that watershed moment between a couple when they could travel comfortably without speaking. He was glad he had begun to open up to Deirdre, though he was still wary of revealing too much of his frustrating indecision.

As an officer he could resign his commission at will. But did he want to? The only other life he knew was Mackenzie Wood Industries. Was he ready to rededicate himself to other duties? He almost wished that, like the enlisted men and women, he had a contractual obligation to serve a certain time, but he didn't. That freedom—the freedom to commit—was driving him crazy.

He wished that he could keep on driving into the night, just to see where the road would take them. It was funny how roads and headlights all looked much the same no matter where you were. It was the person next to you that made the difference.

Soon he was stopped in front of the barracks. He had to nudge a sleepy Deirdre, whose dusky green eyes reminded him of the secluded green spaces of the castle garden.

"Get up, sleepyhead. Tomorrow's Sunday. If you have a yen to attend the nondenominational worship service at the company rec room, you can, and then we can have a picnic in the woods nearby, weather permitting. How about it?" He took the soft mumbling for a "yes," kissed her on the top of her head, then watched as she was admitted by the barracks guard. It was late, nearly midnight, but somehow Jack thought he'd never felt more revitalized.

Deirdre slept the best she had since she'd been in Germany. She awoke to a glorious late fall morning, half-remembering something about a picnic. She glanced at her small wind-up clock: 8:00. She'd better hurry.

She ran into Ann in the large communal bathroom/shower. She also had plans for the day. She was deliberately vague, though, and Deirdre, understanding the need for discretion, didn't press her. For once she didn't envy Ann. At least Deirdre didn't have to hide her relationship with Jack. She realized that she was at that slightly giddy stage of seeing herself as one-half of a couple. Surely there was no more intoxicating and reenergizing excitement in the world—or one more vulnerable to a crashing letdown.

An hour or so later, after gratefully sharing some pastries and coffee that one of the women had brought in, Deirdre heard a knock at the barracks door. As the desk guard was away for a minute, Deirdre answered it.

There stood Jack, dressed in the same pants as the night before but with a more casual bulky sweater and wool deerstalker cap on. Every time she saw him she caught her breath for a moment at his handsomeness, his sturdy well-developed physique, which seemed to be shown off perfectly in whatever he wore, and the brightness of his eyes: alert, intelligent, kind, and ever-so-slightly amused. "Well," he said, "ready for your Sunday picnic in the woods?" He was grinning from ear to ear. "Oh, but there has been a slight change in our plans," he said as the grin disappeared, replaced by a quiet seriousness. "Yes, I'm afraid that a lady who's been a part of my life for some time is going to join us. Is that all right?"

For a minute, Deirdre didn't know whether to laugh or cry. Was he kidding? A lady who was part of his life? Just as she was about to tell him that she had a headache and would take a rain check, she heard a small feminine voice squealing.

"Uncle Jack, Uncle Jack! Look at all these leaves I've swept up!" Deirdre looked behind the door and saw an adorable little girl of about six raking some of the fallen oak and aspen leaves in the courtyard of the barracks and administration building. She looked strikingly like Jack. Her hair was the same dark coppery hue and fell in ringlets down her back. Her skin had the same flushed fairness. As she ran up to the door, Deirdre could see that her eyes were different: Jack's were a unique amber while this little girl's were pale blue.

"Deirdre, I'd like you to meet my niece, Molly. Molly, this is my friend Deirdre, the lady who's going on the picnic with us."

Molly seemed quite unreserved and squealed again with excitement. "Oh, good. Now I have two people to push the swing." She looked at Deirdre with perfect seriousness. "Uncle Jack gets tired of pushing me and never wants to stay long in the forest. Now maybe he'll want to stay longer." Deirdre and Jack looked at each other for a moment and burst out laughing.

"Okay, come on, ladies. Let's get a move on. It looks as if it might rain later, but"—he held up a rattan basket that seemed packed to overflowing with items—"I'm prepared for all contingencies: food, umbrella, picnic blankets, flashlights, cards . . ."

"Cards?" Deirdre laughed.

"Oh, Molly is quite a card shark when it comes to Concentration. Come on."

As the kaserne was not only on the edge of a small village but also across the street from the large state owned forest park where they had stopped the one night, driving was unnecessary. They walked a short distance on a dirt path that ran parallel to the forest, then took a sharp turn to the left. To the right were rows of simple houses, but to the left was the forest proper. After only a few minutes of walking, Deirdre realized that it wasn't just large, it was huge. It truly was a fairytale forest, especially on this sunny, breezy fall day.

Molly kept running ahead, and such was the nature of the dense forest and winding paths, that she would be quickly lost from sight until Jack called her back.

"Don't get too far ahead, Molly," he said.

"But Uncle Jack, I've *been* here before! I know where the swings and tables are!" She was so excited that, having been forced to retreat, she was literally dancing and hopping in circles around Jack and Deirdre.

"I know, I know, but keep in sight, okay?"

Molly reluctantly agreed, then promptly dashed off like a forest sprite.

Jack shook his head with affectionate exasperation.

"She is a lovely little girl," Deirdre said with sincerity.

"Yeah, she is. She's a good kid. Hope you don't mind her tagging along."

"Of course not. And thanks for a wonderful evening. I was so sleepy. I can't remember if I even thanked you when you dropped me off."

"You're welcome, and"—he smiled—"you didn't say much. It was a long day. Not too long, I hope."

"No. In fact, I slept like a log." Deirdre glanced around her. "An appropriate simile, I guess."

"Actually, I didn't know until this morning that Molly would be joining us. My brother and his wife had some business in Brussels and Frankfurt, and dropped her off for a few days. They do that a lot, if they happen to be travelling where I am stationed. The BOQ—that's bachelor officers' quarters to you civilians—has enough room for the occasional visitor. I get home to Oregon so seldom that I enjoy these stints as a baby-sitter. It gives me a chance to know my only niece."

"Your brother and his wife must be very proud of her. She's a charmer."

"Oh, they are, sure. And they're good parents, but I think they sometimes feel guilty about dragging her around so much on family business. But my brother would be too lonely leaving Pat, his wife, and Molly home. Besides, Pat is an important part of the business. She does the books and is very good with the public relations aspect. She's also the linguist in the family, which comes in handy as Mackenzie Wood Industries develops more and more business in Europe and Asia."

"But what about when Molly starts school?"

"Yeah, that's one thing that worries them. She is only five and a half, but she should start next year. I guess they'll cross that bridge when they come to it."

Deirdre felt she was getting to know Jack better as a person, seeing him as doting uncle and concerned brother as well as an officer. She still sensed that something was bothering him, something that he always seemed on the verge of confiding, but never quite being able to do it.

As they walked along the path, Deirdre delighted in the various changes that autumn had already wrought in the forest. Some trees were already golden and flaming red; the leaves floated down on them like the casual blessings of ancient gods. Other trees had not yet changed, and their trembling green leaves seemed indecisive amid the abandon of the fall foliage. And of course there were firs and ferns, whose green promised year-round reminders of the life that pulsed beneath the winter season.

Before she knew it, they were in a small clearing perhaps a mile into the forest. For the first time, Deirdre saw a few other people. An old couple, dressed with old-fashioned formality in somber gray hats, gloves, and topcoats, sat on an elaborately carved bench on the edge of the clearing. They watched the afternoon's activity silently but not sadly, almost as if they were honored guests at a play. There were several groups of families with energetic toddlers or mothers pushing pastel strollers. A scruffy but intellectual-looking young man sat on a mossy log on the side of the clearing, apparently lost in a book. Deirdre thought it looked much the way any park would look in any small town. Still, to her there was a romantic "foreign" aura to the scene. She began to feel as if she were on the verge of a new life—though she could not logically explain why.

Jack placed the basket on the ground as the few tables were already occupied. "Good thing I brought a few of these." He shook out two old plaid blankets and smoothed them over the leaves and twigs, tossing aside a few stones and rotting wood.

Deirdre then knelt on the blankets and together they began to unpack the basket as Molly raced toward the swings. Deirdre's meager breakfast of coffee and rolls made her eye with appreciation the variety of snacks that were tucked into the basket. Packets of cream cheese and butter, boxes of crackers and cookies, a small jar of olives, and some deli meats and cheeses in white paper showed that he must have done some morning shopping. There were also dark blue bottles of mineral water and several cans of a German soda pop, citrus by the look of the stylized lemon on the label. "This looks wonderful, Jack."

He seemed pleased but gestured as if to say, "hey, I can do this blindfolded." Deirdre couldn't help but wonder how many other ladies had been his companion on a romantic lunch in the woods.

"Do you do this often?" She couldn't help herself.

Jack, whether catching the drift of her question or not, answered absently. "No, not really. I never think to come here by myself, and Molly has visited me only twice in the last year."

Deirdre smiled. *Well, I guess that answered that.* She was pleased to think that this was a special moment for him too—or at least a unique moment. She was already beginning to feel proprietary about him. Not necessarily a good thing, if it weren't returned in kind.

But the growling of her stomach made her concentrate on the matter at hand. Jack called Molly, and they all dug in without ceremony, making what Molly called "cracker sandwiches" and thoroughly enjoying the informality of the meal.

After munching all she wanted, Molly asked if she could go back to the swings and the slide, having already made a few fast friends among the other children. Children surmounted language barriers so much better than adults.

Jack pondered the weighty question of "Can I *please* go play?" and then replied, "Why don't we play a round of Concentration first? That will give your food a chance to settle."

Molly appeared to think this adult reasoning far-fetched. "Settle *where,* Uncle Jack? It's already in my stomach. It's not going anywhere."

Jack laughed. "That's the idea. Sit down for a while. Let those cracker sandwiches settle down to your toes." He tickled her feet, causing the serious Molly to finally collapse in a giggling heap on the blanket.

"Okay, okay." Deirdre help to clear a place for the game and laid out the cards. Molly proved to have an astonishing memory, picking up pairs so fast that she was clearly the winner in a short time. She teased Jack when she picked up both pairs of jacks in a row. She held the different versions of the jack up to her uncle, searching for a resemblance.

"I forget, Uncle Jack. What is a jack?" She giggled, and Deirdre wondered if this were some honored ritual, one of those touchstones of common memory that even children needed and cherished.

Jack thought with exaggerated soberness. "Hmm, let's see. I think he is supposed to be the knight who serves the queen. That's why his card is lower than hers."

"What about the king?" Molly pursued. "Is he a grown-up jack?"

"Oh, I don't know. I don't think jacks ever grow up, twinkle toes," Jack teased as he again tickled her feet.

Deirdre watched them with affection, thinking how different he seemed when he let down his guard, as he so clearly did around Molly. Finally, Molly was off to the swings again and Jack lay back on the blanket looking at Deirdre with amusement. "You're very good with her, Jack. I guess I thought someone who was used to giving orders to adult men and women would have trouble relating to children. But you don't."

"Thanks. I enjoy kids." He picked absently at the leaves that had fallen on the blanket. "It's one thing I feel I've missed."

There was silence for a moment, as each thought of comparable gaps in their lives. Finally, Deirdre said, "I know what you mean. I think I'm at the stage in my life where I'm beginning to miss some of the things that I used to think were optional." She looked at him, thinking, *Please don't make me regret opening up to you. Don't misunderstand.*

Jack slowly nodded his head. "You know, I haven't told anyone—and I mean *anyone*—" He swallowed hard, and then said quickly, as if afraid of losing his nerve, "I'm thinking of leaving the Army. There are too many other needs and obligations that are beginning to crowd my life. And too many regrets."

Even after his comments of the previous evening, Deirdre couldn't help but be surprised. She'd never dreamed that this walking advertisement for the U.S. Army would or could imagine a life away from the military. "When would you leave?"

"Well, I don't know. I could formally resign my commission any time, but . . . there are just a lot of things to take into account, and I want to make sure I'm doing it for the right reasons. Please don't mention it to anyone." He shredded a handful of leaves and tossed them aside. "I don't know what I'll do."

Deirdre sat quietly, feeling closer than ever to this complex and constantly surprising man.

They both sat for a moment without talking. The only sound was that of Molly humming to herself. She had tired of the swings when her new little friends left, and was now happily gathering leaves in the cellophane deli bag.

A darkening of sky and strengthening of wind presaged a storm that could break at any moment.

Deirdre was just about to ask whether they should begin to gather up their picnic and head home, when Jack said unexpectedly, "Deirdre, have you ever thought about what you wanted to be doing in five years or so? Where you wanted to live? What would make you happy?"

Deirdre was thrown off-balance by the question. She wasn't sure that anyone, certainly not since she was a grown woman, had ever asked her so directly what she wanted. What *would* make her happy? She thought a moment, and answered honestly. "I've always loved the forest." She stopped and gazed around her. "When I go back I'd like to live some place where I can enjoy this sort of scene a lot, if not everyday. And I guess, as I'd mentioned last night, I'd like to be married, settled, with children. But I have other goals too. I spent a lot of time, money, and energy gaining an education. I want to find some way to use it."

Jack continued to appear lost in his thoughts, but clearly was listening intently to every word she said, thinking over some conflict in his mind. Just as he was about to say something, they both noticed that although the sun still shone, a light, misty rain had begun to fall. They both jumped up and started tossing the remnants of their picnic into the basket. They would be drenched, even with the umbrellas, because the wind had begun to make it a driving rain. Clouds finally smothered the afternoon sun as they ran for cover to a small rustic gazebo of rough-hewn wood, provided no doubt for just such occasions.

Molly seemed delighted with this new dimension to her outing and stood at the opening of the gazebo with one of the blankets draped over her head, dwarfing her small body. She looked like a diminutive tartan ghost. Deirdre and Jack sat on the seat, another blanket thrown behind their shoulders, a few leaves still clinging to it. The rain had become a downpour and they all gazed out into the silent forest. Silent, yet somehow very much alive. Ophidian limbs of oak coiled like wet black snakes to hidden spots in the red leaves. Birch and poplars gave up golden leaves with each heaving gust as if they were languidly undressing themselves. Deirdre felt like a spectator in a box at the theater, watching some occult mystery of nature.

She looked up into Jack's face and asked, "Is it really true that jacks never grow up?"

He looked down into her eyes, his own remarkable honey-colored eyes reflecting the season's golden color, and whispered, "One grows up and lives happily ever after: the jack of hearts."

Anyone watching the scene from afar might have thought it a charming tableau of a small family enjoying a late fall afternoon. And they might have been touched by the tender way that the man turned and kissed the woman for a brief moment, and then continued to gaze at her a long, long time.

Chapter Six

By the time Deirdre's classes were through the first month of a three-month term, she felt pleased with the enthusiasm of most of her students and vindicated in her conviction that on-post college classes were a good idea.

However, she hadn't seen Jack since their picnic with Molly. They had had such a wonderful time that Sunday afternoon. She knew, of course, that his brother and sister-in-law had returned for Molly. No doubt Jack had spent time with them.

But she hated the feeling of not knowing whether this was a potentially serious relationship, one she should nurture with hope and plans, or just a casual friendship forged out of common need and coincidence. Byron's lines came back to her: *"Man's love is of man's life a thing apart; tis woman's whole existence!"* But she *had* an existence! Still, she had to admit that it was an existence that seemed more and more hollow without someone—without Jack. She wished that she could strike that elusive balance between being deeply committed without being wholly dependent. Could love ever be that logical?

Did she love Jack? Could she? Whether yes or no, she had to continue to try to do the best job she could for her classes. Juan, in particular, had a promise that revealed itself more and more as the term progressed. He was in the literature survey course as well as the composition class. His comments on medieval ballads and Shakespearean sonnets were perceptive if not technically correct. He reminded her of what she had once read, that all that was needed to understand Shakespeare was an open mind and an open heart. And one found those in the most unexpected places. An open heart. Why did all thoughts lead to Jack?

Ann tapped on the door and came in. She and Deirdre had developed those subtle but crucial courtesies in being roommates. Respecting each other's space was one of the most valued.

"Hi! Still grading papers? I never dreamed that teachers spent so much time outside of class on grading and stuff. You really earn your pay in ways most of us don't realize."

"Bless you, Ann. Please relay those thoughts to the next disgruntled parent or schoolboard member you meet. I'm just about through."

"Good. How 'bout grabbing a bite before class? We can go directly to class after." Ann smiled and waved a stapled essay in the air. "My first essay! I did a comparison/contrast on the life of the enlisted versus the life of an officer."

"Oh, Ann, you didn't." Deirdre laughed and shuffled the papers into her leather document holder. "Dare I read it out loud in class?"

Laughing, Ann shook her head. "I don't think so. Is the snack bar okay?"

"Sure. It's the best offer I've had in a while—about three weeks to be exact." Realizing how that sounded, she quickly apologized. "Oh, I didn't mean it like that. It's just that—"

Ann cut her off with a wave of the hand. "No explanation necessary. You know, he has been busy. This is the time of year when there is a huge multinational war game about to be-gin. As the CO of the tactical signal unit, not to mention acting battalion CO, he has a lot of pressure to have everything—and I mean everything—exactly coordinated. You have no idea the planning that goes into a few weeks in the field."

"War games?" Deirdre thought that sounded ominous. "You mean like guns?"

"Well, they don't really call them war games, but it is a readiness preparation for that possibility, I guess. And by the way, we call them 'weapons,' not guns. Of course, they're part of the training maneuvers, but all troops have to qualify on the range at least once a year." She smiled. "I'm a certified sharpshooter myself. Anyway, the whole thing is very im-portant, and very time-consuming."

"I guess there's a lot more to being in the military than most civilians realize. Let me grab my purse and sweater, and we'll grab one of those deliciously greasy cheeseburgers at the snack bar."

About an hour later, as the afternoon faded into a cloudy and chill evening, Deirdre and Ann walked to the schoolroom. They were caught up in their conversation as Deirdre opened the door to the room. She literally gasped as she realized no one was there. Not a single soul. It was such a shock that she actually did a double take at the room number, thinking she had walked into the wrong room.

Ann also seemed stunned. "Where is everyone?" Ann asked as she walked into the room and slowly turned a complete circle as if checking to see if someone were hiding in the corner.

"That's what I'd like to know! We're actually five minutes late. Everyone should be here by now."

Slowly, the truth began to sink in for Ann. "Oh, no, I think I understand. I told you that this massive maneuver is scheduled for next week. The CO may have everyone pulling special duty to get ready." She held up her hand in a gesture of resignation. "I guess there's no class tonight."

"Why didn't you know?" Deirdre didn't mean to sound accusatory, but she felt as if the rug had been jerked out from under her.

"Because I'm a short-timer. I'm basically assigned to barracks duty, especially when a field shot or maneuver is going on. I'm low on the totem pole for information of this sort."

"But he can't do this! This class is supposed

to meet tonight. I have assignments, readings, a lecture to give—"

Ann allowed her impatience to show. "Deirdre, like you said, there are things you don't understand fully about the military. This field exercise is important; the CO can, does, and should assure that his company is as ready as he can make it." She paused, and then spoke more quietly. "Look, I'm on your side. I think you're a very good teacher, and they—we—are lucky to have you. But you are a teacher on a military base, and the military comes first. I'm sorry." She turned and walked out, leaving Deirdre feeling as desolate and alone as she had since she had first arrived on the kaserne. Worst of all, she felt betrayed by Jack, as if this were some sort of personal humiliation. She knew that was irrational and childish, but she felt it nonetheless.

Somehow, that feeling of betrayal turned her disappointment in an empty classroom into anger. Rightly or wrongly, she knew whom she was going to blame.

Jack was in his office, sipping a cup of coffee, when he heard the click of heels on the tile floor in the outer office. As these heels had the unmistakable click of civilian shoes, not GI combat boots, he had a pretty good idea of who it was. He sighed to himself, bracing for what he knew would be a tense encounter. He had thought of Deirdre every day since that Sunday afternoon. He had even begun to think in terms of what if . . . Could she ever agree to be a part of his life after the Army? Did he really want that? And now after all those pleasant moments of romantic daydreams, he had to confront her in a sticky moment like this. Still, despite the trepidation, he felt an excitement, an electricity that seemed to charge his mind and body at the thought that he would see her any moment.

The office phone rang, informing him that Ms. Lonagan was here to see him. A second later the door opened.

Jack had remembered her as beautiful, but as she stood there with her black hair windblown, her pale skin colored by anger and the weather, her green eyes glowing with emotion like seawater shot with sun, he was speechless. He felt like a smitten schoolboy as he sat there, frozen for a moment, just taking in the sight of her.

She closed the door, seemingly making an effort not to slam it. With her arms crossed, her breath still coming with an effort through anger, she said slowly, "Nice going, Captain.

You have single-handedly wiped out my class!"

Jack put his cup down, still entranced by the lovely woman who, raw with anger and frustration, evoked both compassion and exasperation.

"Don't be ridiculous. You have to get over this idea, Deirdre, that I am somehow out to sabotage your classes. I told you the first day you arrived that I am all for it, but it cannot, *cannot,* interfere with the primary military duty of this company's personnel. I'm sure you don't realize this, but there is an important NATO maneuver . . ."

"I know, I know. Ann told me. But it doesn't start until next week."

"Right, but preparations are required *this* week. You don't just walk into a class and teach it without some preparations, do you? Well, the same is true in this case. More so."

Deirdre fumed even more over that. Jack realized that he sounded more patronizing than he intended. He leaned back in his chair and rested a boot on the open bottom drawer of his desk. "Deirdre, this is what I was afraid of from the beginning. There is the potential for too much conflict of schedules for education on base to work. You know, everyone has to make sacrifices at some time, and one kind of sacrifice is to postpone certain choices. Anyone who is in the military on active duty right now has, by choice, postponed the choice to pursue an education."

Deirdre could keep silent no longer. "I was supposed to deliver a lecture tonight, not be given one! I realize this is all very easy for you to say, being a dyed-in-the-wool officer. I frankly can't see you leaving the Army, ever."

Jack was stung. She was the one person he had confided in about his possible decision to resign his commission, and now she turned it back on him. What wounded him most of all was that she didn't seem to understand the personal sacrifice that lay behind him—and perhaps before him.

"I asked you to keep that private. I'm sorry you couldn't honor the confidence."

Deirdre glanced at the closed door. "No one can hear us. And I haven't told anyone."

"Since you have brought me into this discussion in a personal way, let me point something out to you. One reason I'm thinking about leaving the military is to go back to my family's business. It's not fair that Ron has had to shoulder that responsibility for so long. I thought that if I went back into it, I could do more of the traveling and he could stay home with his family."

Jack thought Deirdre looked a little disappointed at that. "Oh. I thought that maybe you wanted out of the military to have a family yourself."

"Well, yes, yes, that's it too. The point is, I to some extent gave up a personal life when I joined the Army, and I will sacrifice my training and experience as an officer when I leave the Army to help my family."

Deirdre's eyebrows rose in surprise. "When? You have decided, then?"

Jack was caught off-guard. Had he said "when"? Did he mean it? "Well, no, not really. I haven't decided. I just used that as an example."

"So where does that leave . . . us?" Deirdre asked quietly.

They paused for a moment, each feeling the force of the double meaning. Jack again felt the thrill of looking at her, the lost-in-the-moment emotion of falling in love.

"Can't we compromise? Maybe classes could be by correspondence, at least while the troops are in the field," Jack suggested.

Deirdre looked at him for a long minute. "Well, that would rather negate the need for my presence, wouldn't it? Correspondence courses could be handled through the extension office in Frankfurt—or the State for that matter."

Jack didn't like the direction the conversation was going but he didn't know how to change it.

Deirdre continued. "There is a real need for a teacher here, a living, breathing teacher. Do you know that there are some very bright students, or troops, here?"

Jack commented wryly, "Now who's being patronizing?"

Deirdre looked slightly embarrassed. "You're right. But I meant only that there is a lot of potential here, potential that only a focused education can really open up. Sure, an education two or three years down the road is an option, but why deny them the extra dimension that education can give them *now?*"

This was exactly the sort of "groves of academe" theorizing that annoyed Jack about educational types. And at the moment he was again seeing Deirdre as very much in that category.

Deirdre took his lack of response as tacit agreement and pressed on. "One student, Juan

Rodriquez, is truly gifted in his talent for writing and for analyzing literature."

Jack finally sputtered, "So? So what?" He tried to load the terse question with as much displeasure as he could.

"So, every time he reads a poem or a short story or writes an essay, he is exercising his mind in a way that makes him a different person, however minutely. It's true for everyone, of course, but it is always more obvious in someone who has a talent for a particular discipline. I can give him and all the other students the encouragement, and when needed, the correction that will help change them as people, not just educate them."

Jack sat for a second before he realized that she had stopped talking. The wind flush had gone, the anger had gone, but now she had an even more striking glow about her, the glow of someone who really believed in what she was doing. He admired her for that and he envied her a bit too. And he loved her all the more because of it.

"Do you even know who Juan is?" Deirdre asked.

Again, that stung. "Of course I know who he is. He's our top voice radio operator repairman. Maybe I see an entirely different potential in him, did you think of that?"

"Well, maybe that sums up nicely how hopelessly different we—"

Just then the phone rang. Jack gestured for her to wait, and answered. "Yes, sir. Yes, Colonel." He knew this would be a long conversation. He was just about to ask Deirdre to wait when she turned on her heel and walked out.

As Deirdre slammed the door to Jack's office, she caught a glimpse of his surprised, even hurt, face. *Too bad,* she sulked. How could he be so casual about *her* job? Did he really not care whether she had a reason to stay or not? She walked quickly through the outer office, noticing as she did so that Sgt. Cramer was looking at her suspiciously. What did Deirdre care whether she heard or not? Her opinion of the sergeant, never particularly warm, fell a notch or two.

She walked into the brisk air of the evening and by chance almost literally ran into Juan.

"Juan! I'm glad I saw you. I'm sorry that we won't be able to have class tonight." She noticed the cables he was carrying. He also seemed to be dressed for rough weather in the field. The usual fatigues had been covered by a bulky parka and a cap with ear flaps.

"Ms. Lonagan, how are you? I'm sorry about the class too." He seemed hurried and perhaps a little nervous about being drawn into a conversation about the reason for the cancellation of the class. "We're going to be in the field until just before Thanksgiving. That's at least three weeks' worth of classes." He shrugged in the same gesture of resignation that Ann had used earlier in the evening. He smiled. "I hope I can still continue in the classes. I'm enjoying them both and learning a lot."

"Don't worry about it, Juan. We'll catch up when everyone gets back."

This seemed to reassure him and he went on his way. Her conversation with Juan had cooled her temper a bit, and her pace down the darkened kaserne street slowed. As she contemplated a stop at the snack bar for a hot drink, she heard her name.

"Deirdre! Wait!"

Oh, no, she thought. It was Jack. She really didn't feel like going over the same arguments again. If class was canceled, she just wanted to get some hot cocoa, go back to the barracks, and go to bed.

Jack was slightly out of breath as he caught up to her.

"Deirdre, that call was from brigade. We have a problem. The two female enlisted NCOs who were supposed to operate the voice radio station in the field are out. One has to go back to the States because of a sudden death in the family. The other is in the hospital with pneumonia and a prognosis for a long recuperation." He paused to catch his breath.

Deirdre interjected as an ironic echo of his earlier remark, "So?"

"So, Spec. Shubert is going to have to be the operator. But all other female personnel in this company have been assigned to shot locations. We need at least two women on site. Army policy, and it's absolute. Now, the brigade CO is trying to commandeer another female radio operator from another kaserne, but so far no joy and little hope. We leave in a week..." He trailed off, as if he didn't quite know how to finish.

The point of this conversation suddenly became plain. Deirdre almost laughed. "You mean you want *me* to go to the field?"

Jack gestured as if to say, "it's not as bad as you think." "Look, it would only be for a few days. Obviously, you would not have to actually do anything—just be there."

Deirdre was dumbfounded at the audacity of the request. "But I don't even have a security clearance."

Jack was ready. "Oh, yes you do. Even civilian employees have minimal clearance. What do you think those files are for?" Deirdre remembered their first conversation and how he knew a fair amount about her background.

Jack continued. "True, you don't have a TS, I mean top secret, clearance as most of us have to, but we'll just make sure that you aren't allowed access to sensitive areas: equipment, records, etc." He paused, and seemed to be saying a silent prayer. "Please. Please, Deirdre. If you don't, it is really going to louse up the beginning of this shot."

Deirdre was acutely conscious of the irony of the timing. Scarcely ten minutes earlier he had seemed ready to dismiss her job, her duty, as utterly dispensable, or at least optional. Now he wanted her to help bail him out of *his* work predicament.

Jack, perhaps sensing a crack in her defenses, continued. "There won't be anything to do here anyway. Everyone will be gone to the field, or almost everyone. It'll pass the time, and as I said, it will only be for a few days. How about it?" He smiled his irresistible smile, and said, "Your country calls."

In spite of herself, she grinned. "Do I have to wear fatigues and those awful boots?"

Jack realized he had won the battle, but allowed the loser to save some face. He laughed. "Well, I don't think you want your L. L. Bean corduroys to get mucked up in the field. You can't wear uniform, of course, but we can outfit you with some surplus fatigue pants and a parka. I think a pair of running shoes should be okay, but not a good pair. It will be muddy and wet."

Deirdre, holding her hands up in the resigned gesture that seemed to be obligatory this evening, agreed to be the second female on site.

Chapter Seven

The next week passed in a blur of activity as the various signal companies on the kaserne went through the familiar rituals of preparing for the field. Radios, antennae, and cable lines were packed in military trunks as carefully as if they were fine bone china. Field gear was brought out from duffel bags and missing caps, gloves, and socks were replaced. There was an intensity among both enlisted and officers that Deirdre hadn't noticed before. This, she supposed, was as close as they got to a genuine deployment, and the tension and excitement reflected that. Although she heard some griping in the snack bar or in the barracks common

107

room about the week's separation from creature comforts, she also sensed that the troops anticipated the maneuver as an adventure. Ann had jokingly referred to it as a "camp-out with a mission."

She and Jack hadn't had a chance to see each other; there was simply too much to do. But he had passed her once on the kaserne's main thoroughfare and remarked with a wink, "Don't forget to bring some cards. Maybe we'll find time for a round of Concentration."

The night before the big day, she and Ann had stayed up late polishing boots, though Deirdre hadn't seen the point of cleaning shoes that would be caked with mud by lunch time the next day. "The polishing actually helps to waterproof the boots a little. Sure you don't want to wear a pair?"

"No thanks. I'll stick with my old tennies."

"Okay, but I'm sticking in an old pair for you just in case it's unusually wet or, heaven help us, snowy. That's not likely though."

Early the next morning Deirdre awoke to Ann's hushed voice.

"Deirdre, wake up. We've got to get ready."

Reluctantly, Deirdre dragged herself out of bed. After a quick shower downstairs, she was dressing in hastily procured olive-green fatigue pants and T-shirt as she peppered Ann with questions about what to expect in the field.

"Where do we eat?" Deirdre asked as she pulled on heavy socks to wear under her sloppy shoes.

"Wherever you can find a place to sit down! There's no mess hall, you know. We eat prepackaged meals, usually cans or pouches of a main dish with fruit or chocolate. It's not supposed to be gourmet. The best thing about it is that it makes you long for mess hall food."

"What about, you know, restrooms?"

Ann laughed. "This is the *field,* Deirdre, but we aren't totally back-to-nature. We use a unisex latrine tent."

Deirdre grimaced. "How come you don't seem more upset by this surprise order to go to the field? Aren't you a short-timer?"

"Yeah, but still under Army orders until literally the minute I am discharged. I never liked going to the field, but, well . . . it can have advantages." She smiled slyly.

Of course. Lane, as the company's XO, would be there. This made Deirdre think instinctively of her toiletries. She got up and went to the bedside drawer. After rummaging for cosmetics a minute, she said, "Hey. I wonder where my perfume is."

Ann looked puzzled. "Did you leave it downstairs after showering?"

"No, I never took it out except to apply it or to stick it in my purse. Oh, well." Deirdre could hardly hide the disappointment in her voice. She had spent more than she should have on the small vial of "Magie Noire."

"Well, you surely weren't going to take it to the field?"

"No, but . . ." She held up a handful of her "indispensable" cosmetics: mascara, lipstick, concealer.

Ann shook her head. "For Pete's sake, the last time I went to the field I washed my face in my helmet! It really is ridiculous to waste time on vanity on these occasions."

Deirdre thought it was easy for Ann to say, as she had the fresh-scrubbed looks that required little if any makeup. She always felt that her own coloring looked washed out without some sprucing up. Still, she guessed it would be absurd to traipse through the mud as carefully made up as for a dinner party.

Regretfully, she tossed the makeup back in the drawer. "Well, I guess Jack and everyone else will see me *au naturel,* then. Probably doesn't make any difference anyway."

Ann studied her for a moment. "Deirdre, for

what it's worth, I think Jack really is interested in you—with or without makeup. And I wouldn't let this scheduling conflict with the classes come between you. Just relax, be yourself, and see what comes of it. At least you'll have something to talk about back home. Spending a couple of days in the muddy fields of Germany on a semi-secret communications exercise is a unique experience, to say the least."

After meeting in the transportation yard and milling around for a while, Deirdre now understood the military joke, "Hurry up and wait." The main part of the company convoyed to the site in a combination of "deuce and a half" trucks, jeeps, and special communications vans. Deirdre noticed that, true to his word, Jack had made sure that she was kept away from the crypto-teletype trucks. She rode with Lane in a jeep. Ann rode in one of the large trucks with some of the radio equipment.

"So, Deirdre, it looks like we're going to turn you into a recruit yet!" Lane's pleasantly broad face had the look of a kid on Christmas morning. Clearly, he was in his element.

"Well, I wouldn't go as far as that. But I must say that I'm intrigued by what it's going to be like. How long do you think I'll have to stay?"

Lane thought as he lit a cigarette. "Hard to say. The bridge CO is supposed to be working to find a replacement, but frankly, it probably isn't top priority. Don't worry, though. Jack won't let you languish out there too long."

Deirdre wasn't so sure. Deciding on a change of subject, Deirdre indicated that Ann had confided in her about their relationship. Lane didn't look too pleased at first, but then opened up.

"You know, Deirdre, it's funny how you can be around someone for months and just see them as a friend. Then you're gone for a few months, and *wham!* You suddenly know you're in love. I guess it's just as well that we didn't realize how much we cared for each other before, 'cause I probably wouldn't have wanted to go to OCS. Things have a way of working out. But it has been a hassle and a half to try to develop a serious relationship with someone under the watchful eye of Uncle Sam's eagles, so to speak. And worst is that Cramer." Lane shook his head in mild disgust. "Gee, every time I turn around she seems to be lurking about." He took a drag on his cigarette then looked at the ash that had spilled on his thick padded parka. "I've got to give these up. Ann doesn't approve. Anyway, Cramer gives me the creeps."

Deirdre nodded. "I know what you mean. I had the distinction of receiving a hand-delivered note from her a couple of weeks ago. She started giving me a problem because I had hung a few pictures on the wall. With *nails*. Imagine." They both chuckled.

"Yeah, she's a strange one. So is Dietrich."

"Dietrich?"

"Her German boyfriend. He came to the July Fourth company picnic. He used to be a policeman, I think. Huge fellow with a crew cut. Talk about creepy! But she seems nuts about him. Brought him to the picnic just to show him off, I think." He threw the cigarette out the window. "To each his own, I guess."

During the rest of the two-hour drive they chatted about the States, Jack, Ann, and need-to-know oddities in German customs.

Finally, after passing through a tiny village that looked as if it hadn't changed in two hundred years, Lane observed, "We're only a few clicks from the site."

"A few what?"

"Oh, kilometers—clicks for short."

Sure enough, within ten minutes of bumpy

travel they approached a clearing where the rest of the convoy was already stopped and beginning to unload. The shining excitement came back to Lane's face. "Here we are!"

Lane had quickly located Jack in the HQ tent, reverting to his demeanor as executive officer once he was back in the thick of the site preparations. Deirdre looked around her in amazement as everyone seemed to move quickly and efficiently to do his task. There was a minimum of conversation; the two dozen or so men worked as if they were parts of a larger organism, each with his own brain but also aware that there was a larger intelligence and purpose directing all. Deirdre felt out of place, with no explicit purpose for being on site other than the fact that her gender made her the token second female.

She suddenly thought of Ann, who had been part of the convoy that had left first. She asked a harried-looking PFC where Spec. Shubert's tent was, and was motioned to the edge of the site that was opposite the HQ tent.

As she walked over to it, she continued to be awed by the speed with which tents were pitched, cables strung, antennae laid and hoisted.

She came to the small tent's opening and called tentatively, "Ann?"

"Deirdre! You got here!" Deirdre knew that part of the welcoming excitement in Ann's voice was due to her knowing that Lane had arrived as well. "Come in and see your new digs." She was in good humor.

Deirdre thought the tent looked much like any family's campsite, except perhaps the canvas was a little heavier, a little smellier. Inside there were two cots set up. Two duffel bags lay nearby; one was stuffed with personal items and snacks that Deirdre had seen Ann pack the night before. The other appear to contain Ann's field equipment, which she must have packed in the radio "shack." There were also two sleeping bags rolled up on each cot. An old-fashioned stove with a pipe in the center of the tent was venting smoke through an opening in the "ceiling." Deirdre walked over to it and peered critically at the rusty stove pipe and the blackened and dented sides; it looked like an antique. "Does this thing work?"

"Yes and no. It's an oil stove; the oil barrel is outside. It can get very warm and toasty, if you're hovering over it. Get three feet away, and it's basically a smelly, smoky contraption for warming up a cup of coffee. But most of the time we'll be in the company tent or the communications tents. They're kept much warmer. At night, sleep in your fatigues and a sweater, throw a parka on top of the sleeping bag, and you'll be fine."

Deirdre looked to see if Ann was joking; she wasn't. This was going to be a long two or three days.

As if reading her thoughts, Ann reassured her, "It will only be for a few days. Look on the bright side: it'll make the barracks look like the Ritz!"

Deirdre smiled in spite of her dismay.

Ann continued, a little less sure of herself. "I hate to ask you to help. You've already been a life-saver just being here—and the CO appreciates it more than you know—but I've got some setup duties to do. I'd be glad for a helping hand. Besides, it'll pass the time until dinner. There's not much to do here; you can't exactly go on a nature walk, and it's too cold to stay in here."

"Sure. Why not? Anything to pass the time."

"Thanks. Come on." Ann motioned her outside to a couple of shovels. "See that tent off on the far edge of the site? That's going to be the latrine tent."

Deirdre raised her eyebrows. "Going to be? Going to be *when?*"

Ann chuckled lightly. "When we dig it! Let's get started."

And so Deirdre grabbed a shovel and thought that if someone had told her six months ago that she'd be in the middle of a muddy field in Germany about to dig a latrine, she'd have asked if they needed new medication. Still, she couldn't help but feel happy, excited, alive—because she knew that somewhere on site was Jack.

Late in the afternoon most of the tents and equipment were in place. Various pieces of communication were being tuned and tested, and in some cases, retested. As darkness fell, and the cold, cloudy day became an even colder evening, Ann suggested that she and Deirdre go over to the company tent for dinner. Deirdre had tried to catch a glimpse of Jack all day, but those glimpses were few and far between.

She had enjoyed, though, those brief insights into Jack as commanding officer, directing the men to various tasks, supervising, calmly assuring that all cogs in this wheel moved as they supposed to. He hadn't noticed her except once when he looked up from talking to Lane and caught her staring at him. For a moment, they looked across, if not a crowded room, at least a crowded company area, and time seemed to stop.

He smiled at her in a way that made her feel as if she would melt to an insubstantial puddle right then and there. But then he went back to talking earnestly to Lane, and she recovered. Did time begin then again? Or was it then that her life, her heart, seemed to be put on hold? Didn't someone say that when you fell in love, time didn't stop, it started? Deirdre felt the annoyance of not being able to place the quotation, and had absently wandered off, only to be pleasantly surprised by seeing Juan. *Maybe I'll do "double duty" while I'm here,* she thought with some satisfaction.

But now the hard and thankless job of latrine-digging had made both her and Ann hungry. Inside the warm and bright company tent they found a combination of government-issued MREs (meals-ready-to-eat) and a kind of pot-luck of potato chips, cheese, nuts, candy, dried fruit, and soda that the enlisted men had brought from the base and made a communal snackfest of.

Deirdre had just settled on a wobbly chair

when Jack pulled up a cable trunk and sat next to her.

Jack watched as she poked gingerly at the canned ham and scrambled eggs that had been warmed on the oil stove. "How do you like the Army's cuisine du jour?"

"I'll let you know when I try some." Deirdre put the can down and grabbed some chips and a slice of American cheese from a makeshift platter.

"Seriously, Deirdre, I am very grateful for your being here. I know this isn't your style— or your job—but it is a huge help. Now for the goods good news: Sgt. Cramer has been able to find a replacement for herself on base, so she should be out in two days. You can return with the driver when he brings Cramer."

Strangely, Deirdre was a little let down. She relished the thought of a hot shower and a regular bed in a mere two more days, but it occurred to her that she also would be separated from Jack for at least another three weeks. But she tried to show relief.

"Well, I was rather looking forward to washing my hair in a helmet tomorrow, but I'll just have to get over it."

Jack grinned. "You're a good sport." He rose, and dragged the trunk back to the edge of the tent. "I've got to report to *my* CO at brigade. Talk to you later." He winked as he strode out of the company tent to the communications area, where she was not allowed to go.

Oh, well, she thought. She could always use those cards to play solitaire—solitaire with four jacks. She smiled to herself as she recalled Jack's comment that day in the forest. *"One jack grows up and lives happily ever after: the jack of hearts."*

Her eyes roamed the room, noting the camaraderie of the men who had worked all day and now relaxed with their food. A cassette played some pop music at low volume as the men talked, joked, played cards, or all of the above. Deirdre noted, however, that Juan was sitting by himself, looking rather unhappy. She hadn't had a chance to speak to him earlier in the day.

She put down her plate and walked over. "Juan. Hi." He looked up and smiled weakly. "Are you okay? You look kind of down."

"Oh, it's nothing, Ms. Lonagan. I'm just not feeling too well. Not much sleep last night, I guess."

"It can't be the Army food. It hasn't been long enough for it to work its magic," Deirdre joked, trying to cheer up a clearly out-of-sorts

Juan. "Though I have to admit, it wasn't the most appetizing meal I've ever warmed up on an oil stove. How about some chips and cookies?"

"Oh, no. No, thanks. I'm really not too hungry. Excuse me." He got up walked out, presumably to a barracks tent. Deirdre was worried; he didn't look well.

As he was exiting the tent, Deirdre saw Lane and Ann sitting together, eating. They could be simply two company members discussing the day's events—could be, that is, until one noticed that they were talking softly, their faces closer together than necessary, and, the dead giveaway, their eyes locked on each other's as if they were the only ones present. Was it only because Deirdre was herself in love that she could see it in them so easily? Did she have that deer-in-the-headlights look when she was talking to Jack?

She noticed a couple of the men glanced over at Lane and Ann, then whispered with knowing smiles and nods. For Lane's sake, she hoped they were careful. She decided to do them a favor and make their romantic twosome a threesome.

"Hey, you two, want some company?" Deirdre, with her back to the rest of the tent, winked. Ann and Lane seemed to understand and made room for her on the picnic table bench. "Sure, Deirdre," they responded in unison.

Sure, thought Deirdre.

That night Deirdre slept better than she would have thought possible in the cold, damp tent. Ann was right: remaining fully dressed, with a parka topping, had kept her snug and warm inside the sleeping bag. The hard part was getting out of that warm, flannel cocoon the next morning. Ann had got up first and heated some water on the stove for instant coffee. "We'll have regular brewed coffee later in the com tent, but this will get us started."

Deirdre was never in her life so grateful for lukewarm instant coffee. She had a new appreciation and respect for all those countless days and nights that faceless men and women all over the world slept in cold tents and drank grainy coffee, doing their duty. Maybe some did it because they wanted the GI Bill for education, like Juan. Some did it because they were young and a little lost and wanted time and space to figure out what they wanted to do with their lives. Some, like Lane, had a true calling for it, and worked it like a career, bettering themselves along the way. And some, like Jack, sacrificed other kinds of lives in order to pursue some inner sense of duty. But they all did their job, no matter why they were here. And she would never look at them in the same way again. She drained the aluminum cup of its last powdery dregs and followed Ann to the com tent. Maybe today she could find something useful to do.

In the tent, however, was a scene of controlled intensity, if not panic. Jack and Lane were talking to a PFC with a look of concern. Several other men were rummaging through a supply box.

"What's going on?" Ann asked.

Lane looked up, more serious than Deirdre had ever seen him.

"Rodriguez is sick. Very sick. He got up in the night groaning in excruciating pain. Soon after, he started vomiting. He has been drifting in and out of consciousness for the last hour or two. Seems to have a high fever."

"Oh, poor Juan. What do you think it is? Food poisoning?" Ann asked.

Jack spoke up. "I don't think so. The pain and vomiting could certainly be food poisoning. Even fever is sometimes associated with some kinds of highly irritating bacterial food poisons. But when Rodriguez was still lucid, he said he'd been feeling bad for a few weeks. He had tried to shake it off, thinking it would go away. Food poisoning wouldn't come on like that."

Ann agreed. Deirdre then remembered a friend in grad school who had complained of stomach flu for a few weeks, then suddenly became violently ill. She was rushed to the hospital and operated on just in time. Diagnosis: ruptured appendix. The doctor had told her that she missed dying by minutes, not hours. Deirdre brought up the story now.

Lane and Ann seemed surprised, but not Jack. He nodded grimly. "I was thinking the same thing. As you pointed out, Deirdre, minutes, not hours, may very well count if that's his trouble."

"Is there a medic on site?" Deirdre asked.

The three of them looked at her for a minute in a way that reminded her that she was a civilian, and they were military.

Ann explained. "We don't have that kind of personnel. A medic at every site would be a waste of resources. There is a dispensary on post as well as military hospitals in Frankfurt and Heidelberg, but that's a minimum drive of two hours just to get back to post."

Lane spoke up. "We're not even sure that's what it is."

"Isn't there some way you can at least talk to a doctor or a medic, tell him the symptoms?" Deirdre asked.

"Good idea," Jack replied. He started to walk toward the exit. "I'm going to the voice radio tent to see if I can raise anyone in garrison to patch us through to the dispensary. They always have a doctor on duty there."

As he walked out, one of the NCOs who had been rifling through the supply trunk stood up, holding various bottles of aspirin and upset-stomach remedies. "Do you think any of this would help? One time I had a gut-wrenching case of food poisoning, and this pink stuff helped the, uh, various symptoms."

"Look, I'm not a doctor, but I don't think you should give him anything yet, at least until we're sure it's not something serious. He might need surgery," Deirdre observed. "If you can get him to sip room-temperature ginger ale, that at least won't do any harm. But don't leave him. We don't want him to choke."

The NCO seemed willing to bow to her slightly superior knowledge or at least self-confidence, and giving a single nod, left to tend to Juan in the barracks tent.

Ann, Lane, and Deirdre stood looking at one another, not wanting to betray their worry. Deirdre was especially struck that beneath a professional military exterior, Lane was nervous and worried. *They're all a family in a way,* thought Deirdre. Lane and Jack had the responsibility as officers to look out for the welfare of the troops, but it was clearly more than that too.

Jack reentered the tent slightly out of breath. "I got garrison to patch me through to the dispensary. I described the symptoms to the doc on call, and he agreed that it could be appendicitis." Jack paused and looked at Deirdre as if to say, "you've got some practical knowledge as well as that other stuff floating around in your head." "Doc says Rodriguez should be brought to the dispensary as soon as possible, which would be about two hours unless somebody has a lead foot."

Lane seemed frustrated. "What about a Medevac?"

Jack shook his head. "No. The doc said he's not going to call out a chopper for somebody who might just have a gut ache from a bad sausage."

"Yeah, well, if it was *his* gut aching, ol' Doc might feel different about it!" Lane was not just frustrated, he was angry. "That poor kid is not just feeling a little under the weather. He looks bad, really bad. What if two hours is too long?"

In this mini-drama, Deirdre could clearly see the gap between the officers. Lane was still learning, still too given to react emotionally in some situations. Jack, on the other hand, remained calm and realistic. Years of experience and training had given him an authority that was second nature. Lane would get there eventually.

Patiently, Jack explained. "Lane, the doc is just doing his job. A chopper is a resource, and he can't send one into the field every time one of the troops has a bad night. To be fair to him, I think he knows this is potentially serious. He made no bones about the fact that we should get Juan back to post ASAP. Which I'm going to do right now."

"You?" Lane asked. "Why not send Spec. Jackson or me even?"

"Because I'm going to try to do it a lot faster than two hours, and if I get stopped I can explain to the *polizei* the urgency of the situation. Besides, I can get some more crystals for the voice radio—we cracked a few today when we were testing. You're the ranking officer on site until I get back."

Lane agreed. Jack continued, "It will also be an opportunity for Deirdre to get back to post. I'll come back in the morning with Cramer. That'll save a driver the trip tomorrow."

Deirdre responded quickly, "I'll go help get Juan ready."

Ten minutes later, in a pouring rain, Jack, Deirdre, and a nearly unconscious Juan were in a jeep speeding back to the kaserne. They had managed to prop up Juan in the back with several army blankets and a duffel bag. Deirdre kept an eye on him to make sure he didn't get sick again and choke. Jack was focused on the road with an intensity she had never seen. Though they didn't speak, there was an exciting sense of a shared emergency, a shared duty.

As the jeep sped closer to the post, the rain came down heavier and thicker in the dropping temperatures. *Oh, don't let it snow,* thought Deirdre. The downpour almost seemed to have a life of its own, especially when the nearly freezing rain hit the windshield like tiny dragon paws. She was afraid: afraid for Juan, afraid for Jack, afraid for herself. Then, without warning, the jeep hit a sheet of water that had accumulated on the roadway. The vehicle hydroplaned briefly and as its tires made contact with the road's surface again, Jack lost control. They spun sideways into the oncoming lane; fortunately, no other cars were in either lane. Jack slowly brought the jeep to a standstill. For a moment the only sound was Juan's low moaning in the back and the rain beating on them from all sides. Deirdre was frozen with the thought of their near-miss; she felt as if her heart had tripled in size and was hitting her rib cage like a battering ram. She instinctively sought Jack's face with her eyes, thinking but not saying, *Keep me safe, keep me safe.*

His hand reached out to her and smoothed her hair in a comforting gesture. "Are you okay, Deirdre?" Still unable to speak, she nodded slightly. He turned quickly to check the back. "How you doing, Juan?" It was the first time Deirdre had ever heard him call a troop by his first name. Juan moaned a little, then said hoarsely, "Okay, I'm okay." Without wasting another minute, Jack carefully righted the jeep and they continued on to the kaserne. Deirdre decided that if she ever were in a life-and-death emergency, Jack was the man—the tall, complex, wry-humored man—she'd want with her.

*   *   *

An hour and a half later, Jack, Deirdre, and Juan pulled into the emergency lane of the kaserne's dispensary. Two medics wheeled a gurney out and placed Juan on it with no-nonsense efficiency. Jack leaned against the post, looking weary for the first time. Deirdre walked over to him and without a word he wrapped his arms around her. He just held her for a minute, rubbing his hands over her shoulders, breathing into her hair. "Thanks again, Deirdre. Darling Deirdre." She looked up into his golden eyes, and he gazed back as if he would escape into her very soul if he could. "Darling Deirdre." He repeated her name the way he had that first time, as if it were a mystical password, a password to her very essence.

"I'm here, Jack, I'm here." And then they seemed to merge into one as he kissed her.

Chapter Eight

Two days later Deirdre was getting ready to catch a ride with one of the NCOs and visit Juan in the military hospital in Heidelberg. The dispensary medics had rushed him there just in time. Just as with her friend in college, an appendectomy had been performed on a highly inflamed appendix that had been on the verge of rupturing. Deirdre shuddered when she thought how close Juan had come to dying.

Jack had spent the night on post and then taken Sgt. Cramer back the next morning. Deirdre had felt like a fog had enveloped her ever since. She felt such a confusing mix of emotions, contradictory emotions. She was beginning to enjoy her teaching job, but was doubting whether she could really be helpful in a tactical military unit. She was beginning to—no, she was already there: she was in love with Jack. But what possible future could she have with a slightly arrogant, independently rich military man who was tied by obligation to both the Army and family? A trip to visit the recuperating Juan would help her take her focus off herself for a change. Certainly the kaserne offered no diversions. It was eerily like a ghost town when so much of the garrison was in the field.

While she went through her nightstand looking for a pin for her scarf that she could have sworn had been placed in the Wedgwood box, she thought uneasily of how many things— small items—had gone missing in the last few weeks. She hated to think of anyone in the barracks being a minor thief, but she knew she wasn't *that* careless or absentminded with her belongings. For the moment, though, she would rather accuse herself than someone else. And who would she accuse anyway?

Just as she was going down the stairs, looking forward to a day in town, she almost knocked over Ann, who was coming up the stairs in obvious preoccupation.

"Ann! What are you doing back?"

Ann looked as if she were mentally "landing" from outer space. "Hmm? Oh, Deirdre. I just . . . asked to come back early. Cramer is still on site and they got another voice radio operator from another company within brigade to take over for me. She also is a woman, so that took care of two birds, so to speak." Ann smiled faintly and continued up the stairs.

Deirdre turned and looked after her, astonished at her friend's demeanor; she looked pale and shaken.

"Ann? Are you okay?" Ann continued up the stairs, but nodded her head.

"Yeah, I'm okay," she muttered.

Deirdre felt torn between pursuing her gut instinct that something was definitely not okay, and going ahead with the plan to go to Heidelberg. She made a quick decision. She ran down to the barracks guard on duty and told her to inform Sgt. Martin that she wouldn't be able to go with him to see Juan. She handed the guard a few paperbacks bound with a rubber band.

"Tell Sgt. Martin to give these to Juan. They're to help him pass the time, just a few of my favorite mystery writers. Thanks." She then turned and ran back up the stairs.

She walked down the hallway to her and Ann's room and rapped lightly on the door. "Ann?" She walked in.

Ann seemed surprised, and not entirely pleasantly, to see her.

"Deirdre, I said I was okay." She sounded irritable, totally unlike herself. She was digging furiously in one of the dresser drawers they shared. "Did you take that pale blue scarf of mine?" It was almost an accusation.

"Of course not! 'Take it? What's that supposed to mean? By the way, I'm missing a scarf pin as well as my perfume. Also, my only half-slip, a good silk one, isn't in the drawer where it should be."

Ann stopped her digging and looked at Deirdre for a few seconds. "Oh. Hey, I didn't mean anything, it's just that I've noticed a couple of things missing lately. Normally I wouldn't give it much thought, but I'm . . . a bit on edge, I guess." She tossed her hands in the air in a gesture of frustration and plunked down on the bed. "No offense."

"None taken. Now why don't you tell me what's really bothering you. Why did you ask to come back early? I didn't know you could even do that."

"Well, normally, I wouldn't have, couldn't

have, but since I am a short-timer, when this radio operator from another company within the brigade came through, I thought well, I might as well come back to start to straighten things out. I'm going to be discharged in six weeks, you know. I wasn't really supposed to be on this shot anyway."

Deirdre nodded thoughtfully, studying her friend. Something wasn't right, but if Ann didn't want to talk about it she couldn't force it. Since she was probably too late to catch Sgt. Martin, she might as well go to the PX. "Need anything at the PX? I thought I'd get another bottle of perfume and a few other things."

Ann shook her head, already back to shifting things around in her dresser, either actively looking for something or trying to just occupy herself. "No thanks. See you later."

Deirdre felt as if she had been dismissed, but had experienced that kind of mood herself.

When she returned a couple of hours later, Ann was sitting at their shared desk with a calculator and her bank book. She seemed startled. "Back already?"

"It's been two hours." Deirdre glanced at the bank book. "I seem to never be able to balance my account either. I loved a sweatshirt I saw once: 'How can I be overdrawn when I still

have checks?' " Deirdre laughed. Ann just so-
berly stared at her statement.

"I hate to ask, but could you loan me a little
'til the end of the month?" Ann didn't even
look her in the eye as she asked what was
clearly a difficult question.

"Sure. How much?"

"Well, I don't know, I guess, well, would
five hundred dollars be too much?"

Deirdre hoped she had concealed her surprise—and dismay. She had the five hundred
dollars but not much more. It would be lean
days until the end of the month. "Five hundred? No problem. I can lend it to you." There
was an awkward pause as Deirdre debated
whether Ann was a good-enough friend for her
to ask why she needed it. But if she was close
enough to lend such a significant sum, she was
close enough to inquire.

"May I ask if there is a special need? Is there
any problem?"

Again a long silence ensued as Ann seemed
divided as to whether she should confide. She
turned toward the door as if to ascertain that it
was closed. Then she motioned for Deirdre to
sit on the edge of the bed near the desk.

"I wasn't completely up front about why I
came back from the field." Deirdre nodded

sympathetically. "Yesterday when the CO came back with Cramer"—here Ann's mouth seemed to harden subconsciously—"that witch. Anyway, Lane and I were in our tent, yours and mine, sitting on the cot, talking." Ann looked at Deirdre almost innocently. "You know, we're going to go ahead and get married the middle of December, after I'm discharged. Just a simple ceremony in a small church in Neuberg. So, we had been talking, and he just leaned over and kissed me lightly. Just then Cramer walked in."

Deirdre groaned. Even though it seemed absurd to think that two adults could not exchange an innocent kiss, she had been around the military enough in the past month or so to realize that special rules applied—rules that if broken could have a profound effect on a young officer's career. She supposed that those rules had a good purpose, theoretically, but they didn't seem to be serving a good purpose right now.

Ann continued. "Lane and I were numb. We just looked at each other, then at her. She, of course, was enjoying every minute of it. I thought, great, she'll squeal to the CO before we can say boo. Cramer gave that half-smile that makes her look like a lizard and walked out."

"Oh, Ann, I'm sorry. What happened? Did Jack find out?"

Ann shook her head. "No, not yet anyway. That's where you come in."

At Deirdre's puzzled look, Ann smiled. "The money."

Deirdre was still in the dark. "What does the money have to do with it?"

Ann raised her eyebrows cynically. "Can't you guess? I guess I was a bit naive too. But it suddenly fit in: how Cramer was able to go to places like the Inn, or take weekend vacations over the border in Strasbourg or Paris, how she was able to drive a Mercedes."

"She drives a *Mercedes?* How in the world can she afford it?"

"Exactly. If anyone asked, she'd say it was her boyfriend's, Dietrich's."

"Lane told me about him. He said he was rather creepy."

"He is. And, as far as anyone knows, with no gainful employment. I'm not the only one who has suspected that he might be into the black market in some way."

"Black market?" Deirdre hoped she didn't sound as shocked as she felt.

Ann smiled ruefully. "Deirdre, you *are* even more naive than I am. Of course, there is a thriving black market in the general area. For a number of reasons, but it's not unknown for inexpensive cigs and booze from Uncle Sam's store to end up on the street, resold for mutual profit."

"Isn't that illegal?"

"Of course! That's why it's a black market! Anyway, I found out yesterday that there is another avenue of income for the odd couple: blackmail."

Now Deirdre didn't even bother to hide her shock. "Blackmail? You mean she threatened you with blackmail about Lane?"

"That's right. Of course, I have nothing to lose, but Lane does and she knows it. I think she would love to destroy his career, our relationship, whatever—but she is even more motivated by greed. She hinted that I wasn't the first one who become a victim of her scheming."

"You don't mean Lane has had other girlfriends?" As soon as she said it, Deirdre regretted it.

Ann looked hurt. "No, no. That's not it. She meant that she had used damaging information on other people in the company to get them to pay up."

"How much could a low-level enlisted pay to a blackmailer?" Deirdre thought this was sounding more and more disturbing and even unreal.

"Not much. But who knows what her boyfriend might be up to. Even you must know that drugs are a problem—and a profit—everywhere."

"Okay, so Cramer asked you for the five hundred dollars?"

Ann started to cry. "Yes. She said if I didn't pay, she'd go to the CO, even to brigade. I told her I didn't have money. I'm not rich; neither is Lane. But she said that for now five hundred would do."

"For now? Oh, Ann, you can't let yourself be trapped in such a vicious scheme."

"I can't *not* let myself be trapped!" She reached for a tissue. "I would gladly pay it to protect Lane. Besides, once we're married, it won't matter. But if she squeals before then, Lane could be transferred, at the very least. He would almost certainly be disciplined in some way as well. Believe me, it's easier to just pay and shut up." Ann's sobs had receded to sniffling, with anger surfacing now and again like a diver for air. "I guess that's kind of cowardly, isn't it?"

"You're protecting something you care about and love. That's not cowardly. I think that's rather brave, actually."

Ann smiled finally. "Thanks. I feel better already."

"Let's get a taxi and go to the bank at the PX. I'll make that withdrawal, and you can put this behind you."

Deirdre and Ann conducted their business at the PX complex and returned to the barracks. Ann was almost pathetically grateful for the money and promised Deirdre that she would pay her back by the first of the year, after she and Lane were married.

"Deirdre, Lane does *not* know about Cramer's threats. He was embarrassed and worried when she saw us in the tent, but he doesn't really think she'll say anything. Cramer was too smart to go to him. She knows that he would have turned her in for the blackmail attempt, no matter what it cost him."

"Of course, I should have known. I'm still not sure that you're doing the right thing, but I know you're doing it for the right reasons."

Ann smiled. "Yeah, I know. Cramer knew

that too. She knew I'd do whatever I had to do to protect Lane."

As they were talking, they heard Cramer's voice in the hallway, yelling at one of the women who had left an ironing board up in the common room. Ann rolled her eyes. "What's she doing back? Maybe she got lucky and came back on a shower run. Either that or she's here to collect on her threat. Look, maybe I'd better talk to her alone and give her the money. I just want to get it over with."

"Good idea. I don't really want to have to talk to her anyway."

Deirdre opened the door and stepped into the hallway. Cramer glanced up, then did a double take and quickly walked down the stairs.

Ann had also stepped out into the hall and saw Cramer's reaction. They looked at each other, puzzled. "It's almost as if she was avoiding me," Deirdre said. They shrugged their shoulders and said in unison, "Whatever."

"I'm going to go to the library for a while. Maybe we could get some groceries at the little shop in Neuberg and have cold cuts here later. I'm about burned out on snack bar meals."

"Sure. I've got some preliminary packing to do. Come back whenever you're ready."

Deirdre walked to the two-story post library,

noticing as she went how much the season had turned since her arrival at the end of September. The sky was a dense milky white, the clouds so heavy and unrelieved that the sun was a dim glow overhead. Deirdre thought it looked like a huge baroque pearl whose weak luster was only a reflected light from worlds away.

The library was never exactly crowded, but now it was deserted because of the maneuvers. Deirdre browsed through the old-fashioned white oak card catalogue, then sat down with a book near a window on the top floor. She could see the company HQ from here.

After a half-hour or so, she glanced up and realized that a jeep was parked in front. Had Jack returned? Maybe he and Cramer had driven back together.

She decided to walk over to HQ. When she walked into the anteroom she could see Cramer at her desk, and she almost walked out again, but Cramer glanced up. Too late. Deirdre glowered at her as she walked into the main office. Cramer, who had always been so smugly superior, looked flustered, just as she had earlier in the barracks hallway. She quickly grabbed the papers and log books she had been working on, shoved them into a plastic pouch, and scooted past Deirdre with her head down. *Thank you, Cramer, for acting every bit the weasel you are*, she thought.

Unfortunately, Jack was not in his office, as a quick peak in the darkened inner office revealed. Only one member of the HQ staff had been left behind, a PFC who was also in one of her classes.

"Hi, Ms. Lonagan. Can I help you with something?"

"No, not really. I was just wondering if Jack, that is, if Capt. Mackenzie had returned from the field?"

"No, ma'am. Since Cap'n was in garrison yesterday, I don't expect him back till the weekend. If it's important, I can reach him in the field on the voice radio."

"No, no, don't do that. Nothing important."

"Sorry, ma'am."

"No problem." She turned to walk out when she noticed a familiar fragrance in the air. She looked around. No one else was present except the PFC and her, and she didn't think that he was wearing—"Maggie Noire"! Of course. That's how her precious vial had disappeared! The replacement bottle that she had bought that morning was still in its cellophane wrapping. Cramer knew that Deirdre would recognize her own perfume, especially one as unusual as that. Apparently Cramer's greed for material goods didn't stop with acquiring them through ill-gotten profit; she sometimes, it seemed, simply stole what she wanted. That would explain a lot: not only Deirdre's missing perfume and pin, but Ann's scarf as well. Who knew how many people had missed small items from time to time and had just shrugged it off?

She hoped that Cramer hadn't gone back yet. Perhaps she was still at the barracks.

Deirdre ran from HQ to the barracks. She noticed the jeep was now parked in front of the barracks by the painted chain fence that separated the road from the barracks yard.

She opened the door, waved off the greeting of the barracks guard, and dashed up the stairs.

As she ran down the hall, she could hear a muttering of voices from her and Ann's room. She pushed the ajar door open wide, then leaned with nonchalance against the doorjamb. Ann was just counting out the twenty-dollar bills that had so recently been withdrawn from Deirdre's account. Cramer looked on with such greedy self-absorption that she didn't notice Deirdre at the door.

"Well, well. Payday, eh, Sgt. Cramer? But what I can't figure out is why you need the cash when you can steal everything you want. Or should it be the other way around? Why steal perfume, scarves, jewelry, when you can drain a fellow troop's bank balance?" Deirdre worked to control her disgust. She knew she had Cramer, but she was still curious to see how the unpleasant little creep would respond.

Ann looked surprised, and kept turning her head from Deirdre to Cramer, as if she were trying to figure out where the joke was. Cramer registered total shock, looking almost as if she would faint.

Finally, Ann spoke. "Deirdre, do you think *Cramer* has been stealing our stuff?" She turned to Cramer. *"You're* the barracks rat?"

"Barracks rat?" Deirdre asked.

Now Ann was gaining self-confidence as each passing second brought home how the tables had just turned. "Sure. We all had known about it for some time, that someone had to be a thief. Too many other girls would come up missing items. I had had my suspicions, but no one ever had any evidence. How did you find out, Deirdre?"

"Simple. Cramer was foolish enough to wear the perfume she stole from me. I noticed it just now when she walked past me at HQ." She turned to Cramer. "You should have saved it for those special evenings with Dietrich at the Inn or those trips across the border."

Ann barked a short laugh. "Well, I'll be . . . Deirdre, shall we tell the CO so the MPs can search her room for the goods? Or do you think that's more a matter for the Criminal Investigation Division?"

"Oh, you mean the Army's version of the FBI?" Deirdre thought with mock seriousness. "Frankly, I think we'll have to talk to Jack first. That's the chain of command, isn't it, Ann?"

At this point, Cramer, who had been following the conversation with increasing panic, broke in.

"Okay, okay! I'll give the stuff back!" She looked at Ann. "And you don't have to pay me."

Ann snorted. "Oh, that's really big of you, Cramer. Look, you *will* give *all* the stuff back to everyone. That's a given. You can discreetly start a lost and found and then miraculously announce that your lost-and-found box has turned up with every item that's gone missing. The only question is, should we still turn you over to the CO?" Ann crossed her arms and squinted at Cramer. "By the way, did your boyfriend put you up to this?"

Cramer was genuinely surprised. "Dietrich? What's he got to do with it?"

"Oh, come on. He has no visible means of support but according to you drives a Mercedes."

"Dietrich has nothing to do with this! He lost his job in the *polizei* when he was wounded on duty. He got a disability payment in one lump sum. Now he works part-time as a security consultant for one of the local hightech firms. He really does drive a Mercedes—with money he's earned and saved. The same money he uses when he takes me out. I guess in a way that's why I stole things, just little things. I wanted to have nice stuff to impress him. And the blackmail—I just did that a few times. The others were NCOs, three in all, who were cheating on their wives. They've all gone back to the States, or I'd give them back the money. I swear I would!"

For the first time a note of pitiful pleading entered Cramer's voice. "Please, please don't let this go farther. I'm going to get out in another six months. I'm getting a 'European out' so I can stay in Germany with Dietrich. Don't louse it up for me."

Deirdre thought Ann had almost started to look sympathetic to Cramer until the last part of her plea for mercy. *"Me* louse it up? You're the only louse—or rat—around here. And just because your boyfriend has a little money doesn't mean you have to impress him by breaking the law. The petty thefts don't bother me as much as the betrayal of your fellow enlisted. Unfortunately, at this point, you probably couldn't return the money without causing more problems for innocent people. But you *will* give back those things you stole. And if I *ever* hear that you're putting the squeeze on anyone for any reason, I'll go to the CO so fast your eyeballs will spin in their sockets. Understand?"

Cramer seemed so relieved to realize that she was off the hook for criminal charges and a dishonorable discharge, she nodded her head with enthusiastic energy. "Sure, Shubert. Whatever you say." She started for the door.

"Cramer!" Ann tossed an empty cardboard box she was going to use for packing. "Go write LOST & FOUND on this. It had better be full by tomorrow morning."

For the first time, Deirdre saw Cramer actually smile.

"You bet." And she left. It occurred to Deirdre that she might have just witnessed one of the few times when a Specialist Fourth Class gave a direct order to a Sergeant.

After she closed the door, Ann handed Deirdre her five hundred dollars. "I knew I'd pay this back soon, but I didn't think it would be this soon!" They laughed with genuine relief. "Come on. Let's go get some cold cuts for dinner."

"Sure. By the way, do you believe her about Dietrich?"

Ann thought a moment. "Yeah, I think I do. She seemed really, really worried that he would find out about this. That seemed to bother her more than our going to the CO."

"I thought so too. But what about the black market, his general creepiness?"

"Oh, make no mistake: there's a black market, here as everywhere. But I guess we were wrong about Dietrich. Language can be a big barrier to understanding people sometime. I think I felt a little guilty about that. Anyway, what's the phrase, 'all's well that ends well'?" Again, they laughed as they closed the door behind them.

Chapter Nine

The three weeks after the Cramer incident passed slowly, partly because Jack had not come back from the field during that time. Lane returned several times, however, once bearing a sealed letter from Jack:

Dear Deirdre,
Sorry I won't get back until the end of the shot.
Thanks again for your help. Looking forward
to seeing you soon.

Jack

She had read, folded, unfolded, and reread the note a dozen times. *"Thanks again for your help"? "Looking forward to seeing you soon"?* It could have been a casual bread-and-butter thank-you note to a mere acquaintance. She thought back to what Ann had said about Dietrich, about language being a barrier. She decided that two people could speak the same language and still have a language barrier.

Ironically, she had something of a language barrier with her students too: she couldn't speak to them because she hadn't seen them. She still met her classes for form's sake, but there were at most two or three at each class meeting. Other students had contacted her and sent, by friend or interpost mail, essays and assignments. Deirdre couldn't help but feel that Jack had been proven right: she was now teaching exactly the kind of class that Jack said worked best. Perhaps correspondence courses were the only option for a tactical military unit.

The one bright spot in the past few weeks had been helping Ann with her wedding plans. She'd asked Deirdre to be maid of honor at the small, simple ceremony that would be performed in a two-hundred-year-old chapel in Neuberg by a German pastor. Jack didn't know it yet, but he was going to be best man. As soon as Ann was discharged, Lane planned to tell Jack everything.

And now, just a few days before Thanksgiving, the shot was finally over. The convoys that had left three weeks earlier now rolled back onto post, much the worse for wear. The neat "strack" troops who had exited the garrison's gates with high-energy anticipation now returned dirty, tired, cold, and ready for a mess hall turkey dinner with all the fixings.

Deirdre knew that Jack had to be in the company HQ. Ann said that both he and Lane had been in staff meetings at brigade HQ, but they were back on the kaserne now. She could wait no longer to see him. She dreaded what she knew she had to say to him, but she felt drawn like a plant to a sunny window. She decided to used the pretext of inquiring about a student who hadn't been in touch since the maneuver had started. She knew that Jack and she were at the stage where pretexts shouldn't be necessary, but she instinctively protected her vulnerability. Did it matter anymore?

As soon as she walked into the HQ outer office, she spotted Cramer working at her desk. Cramer looked up briefly, then studiously avoided making eye contact. She had been very subdued since the confrontation with Ann and Deirdre. Deirdre smiled to herself: the rat had become a mouse. Cramer no doubt was biding her time until her discharge date, which was in the spring. The PFC at the other desk also looked up inquisitively. Deirdre asked if the CO was in.

"Sure thing, ma'am." The PFC was Southern and she wondered if he would say "ma'am" even if he weren't military-trained. "Wait just a sec, please, ma'am." He went into Jack's office and closed the door. *He must be busy,* Deirdre thought.

She stood waiting, remembering that morning all those weeks ago when she had first come into this office. It had all seemed so foreign then. Even though she understood far more about the military's rules and lingo, she felt she still knew nothing about its essence— or Jack's. What, ultimately, did he want? Had there ever been any hope for them, or had she been fooling herself all along?

"Ms. Lonagan!" She turned and saw Juan coming from the anteroom. Still pale and weak, he nonetheless seemed to have recovered amazingly well from his appendectomy.

He took her hand, smiling broadly. "How nice to see you!"

"Juan, it's so nice to see *you*. How are you feeling?"

"Pretty well! This is my first day back. I'm

only supposed to have desk duty until after Christmas, but I'm doing fine. And I want to thank you for your help that night." He gave a low whistle. "That was close. Thanks again."

"Nothing to it. I'm just glad you're okay."

A frown creased his brow. "I've missed so many classes though."

"Everyone has. Don't worry about it. We'll meet next week and catch up as best we can. You'll do fine."

Reassured, he smiled. "Oh, thanks. These classes have ben so great for me. I've learned so much." He then turned his attention to depositing a packet of forms on Cramer's desk. "See you next week, Ms. Lonagaan. I'm keeping up with my assignments, so you won't be disappointed."

Deirdre nodded. "Okay, Juan. 'Bye." Just then she realized that the PFC had opened the door to Jack's inner office. Jack was standing by his desk, watching her and Juan—mostly her—with a big smile spread across his handsome face. The PFC returned to his desk. "You can go in, Ms. Lonagan."

"Thanks." She walked in.

"Deirdre!" His pleasure in seeing her was almost pathetic except that it was matched so closely by her own joy in seeing him. But hers was a mixed joy. He pulled a chair close to the desk. "I was planning to come over later to see if you wanted to have lunch, or better yet, dinner. At the Inn? Anyway, come in and sit down." With automatic courtesy he adjusted the chair for her in front of the desk.

"How did the, uh, field shot go?" Deirdre was still getting used to some of the terminology.

"It went well, very well. Lane and I were at brigade yesterday and this morning. The colonel was pleased, so I am pleased. That is the way of the military. And thanks again for pitching in."

Deirdre shrugged. "It was only for a day."

"But it allowed us to get the exercise started on time. I'm grateful." He smiled in that way that seemed to transfix her. When she looked into his eyes she felt that a secret window flew open in her soul. She knew the window looked out on a whole world of possibilities that both excited and frightened her. Was that the sixth sense that Jack was talking about that evening at Heidelberg Castle? Whether it was a primeval response or not, somehow she knew that to look at him was to be liberated, to look away was to be imprisoned. How could she ever bear to be away from him? How did she have any choice?

Almost as much to break the spell of his eyes and smile, she blurted out, "I don't think I'm going to offer another term of classes when this one is finished."

Jack's good humor slowly faded to puzzlement. "What do you mean? Are you going to offer them on the other post? I guess that would be a good idea. They do have a large number of troops over there, and I assume that . . ."

"That's not what I meant. I've decided that you were right. I can see now that classes for active duty military, at least in this kind of unit, are best done through correspondence courses." There, she'd said it. Couldn't take it back now.

Jack's questioning look metamorphosed to outright dismay. "I was wrong about that."

"Wrong?" Deirdre didn't know if she should laugh or cry. "How can you say that you were wrong? So far, nearly half of my class meetings have been ghostly—just a few faint messages from the frontier when students find time to scribble an essay." Deirdre had intended to sound sarcastic, but somehow it hit close to home, and she realized she was near

tears. "I've spent most of my time here in the last month going for walks, eating lousy hamburgers in the snack bar, feeling like I was in a place where I had no purpose! No, correction. I did have one glorious purpose on one occasion: to dig a latrine!" By this point her voice was shaking and she was pointing her finger in the air for emphasis. She hated it when she got like this. She hoped Jack would think the emotion was anger and not what it really was: despair—despair at knowing she would be leaving for home after the first of the year.

Jack appeared stunned, as if he was wracked by bewildering, contrasting emotions himself: anger, surprise, sympathy. Perhaps a bit of despair as well? Deirdre wondered.

"I thought you said you had a year-long contract."

"I do, but I can get out of it. As long as I finish this term, which I have every intention of doing."

"I see, then you can just throw aside the people who trusted and counted on you, is that it?" His voice was thickening with a rising anger.

"Excuse me, but I don't throw aside anyone. But your general point is well taken." She was angered by his anger, and it had allowed her to take control of her more romantic feelings.

"Yes, I will tell my supervisor in Frankfurt that I have not . . . adapted as well as I thought I would. And that I want to go home."

Silence. Then, "You want to go home." Jack mocked her petulance. "Sorry, I thought you were an adult, an independent, intelligent, educated woman who a few months ago sat in that same chair and told me, passionately and persuasively, why people in any circumstances deserved the chance to better themselves."

"Persuasively? I didn't appear to be too successful in persuading you, did I?"

"How do you know? I have begun to think that you were right. In fact, this latest maneuver proved it to me. I saw how the troops in the field would spend some of their free time doing assignments for you. Yeah, they still played cards, had a few beers, and listened to music. But having something else to work on, some other stimulus for their minds rather than just the military, well, it seemed to be a morale booster. I saw some of that just now with Rodriguez. Do you know that when he was in the hospital, the first thing he asked for the day after his surgery was his literature book?" Jack shook his head at the recollection. "I would never have believed it. I do think that having you on post, a living, breathing teacher, makes the difference. And now you're quitting!" The annoyance that had dissipated slightly was back now in full force.

"Well, you should make up your mind, Captain. Maybe a little more morale-boosting directed toward *me* would have prevented me from coming to this decision." Deirdre found that her voice that had shaken with frustration a moment earlier was strengthened from her indignation at Jack's ironic about-face. "Besides, I think it's hypocritical of you to lecture me about quitting when you're planning on doing the same."

She immediately regretted saying it: Jack looked as if she had physically slapped him. For a moment that felt like an eternity, he said nothing. Then, very quietly, he said, "If I resign my commission, Deirdre, it will be because I've felt at times over the last decade that I had quit my family." He paused. "I wasn't there for my wife all those years ago. I don't think it would've made a difference: we were too young. But I still felt I let her down in some way when I had to return to West Point after our wedding. I wasn't there for my dad when he died even though I knew he was dying. I kept thinking, after this week, after the next field shot, after the next inspection. Then it was too late. I wasn't there when my mom died either. I wasn't there when my niece was born. I haven't been there as my brother has struggled with the tremendous commitment that the business requires." He took a deep breath. "I hate to sound self-righteous, Deirdre, but if I quit the Army it will be to commit myself to something else. What are *you* going to commit yourself to?" His anger had now completely evaporated like a mist on a hot summer morning. She could understand now the conflict that had always seemed just beneath the surface, the holding back that she hadn't been able to grasp.

Only now it was too late. They both sat for a moment, looking at each other. It was one of those moments that, once reached, cannot be forded easily, if at all. She felt that window in her soul closing. Deirdre got up to leave.

"Dinner?" Jack asked weakly. But he and Deirdre both knew that again, some subtle yet unmistakable change had occurred in their relationship: two steps forward, three steps back.

Deirdre shook her head without stopping or turning around. "No thanks." And she was gone.

* * *

Deirdre had never felt so low in her life as she did on that Thanksgiving. Classes had been canceled for the holiday. She was trying to read a book, trying to keep herself from slipping deeper into her own personal limbo of frustration and self-accusation. Was she making the right decision?

Jack had sent a note a few hours after their disastrous meeting in his office:

Deirdre,
Please talk to me. I want to discuss something important with you. Please.

Jack

She had sent a one-sentence refusal. What was there to talk about? She had let herself fall in love with a man who had too many other commitments. Besides, they had a clash of personalities, didn't they? His dry humor, forthright opinions, occasional arrogance, could all be exasperating. But that was part of the thrill, wasn't it? Those intellectual and emotional sparks kept her on her toes!

It was no use. As hard as she tried, she couldn't ignore the fact that Jack, for her, was close to perfect. And his few imperfections endeared him to her all the more.

She glanced down at the book she was reading. She had been on the same page for fifteen minutes. She closed her eyes briefly, hoping to still the chaos that engulfed her thoughts and feelings.

She opened her eyes reluctantly and watched Ann packing clothes and small personal items. Her "European out" was imminent. Partly at the prospect of being a civilian again, partly at the prospect of being Lane's wife, Ann glowed these days with happiness and a sure sense of her future. Deirdre was back to the envy she had felt for her at the beginning. No, not envy. Ann was a good friend now, but she at least felt the lack of that almost tangible joy that Ann so clearly reflected.

Ann stopped humming and asked, "Deirdre, why don't you come to the mess hall for dinner with Lane and me? A lot of the enlisted and the officers have Thanksgiving later with their families and invite German friends, but almost everyone stops in at the mess hall just as a social gathering. Come on. It's pretty good. They have all the traditional trimmings. At least one should be a favorite. Mine is cranberry relish—and there aren't too many ways even the Army can mess that up! How about it?" Ann was so encapsulated by her own well-being that she was oblivious to anyone else's mood. But Deirdre didn't blame her. She wished that she were so encapsulated.

"Thanks, Ann, but I think I'll just stay here and read."

Ann finally realized something was wrong. "You can't stay here," she said gently. "Besides, Jack will probably stop by the hall. I don't want to pry, but I notice you haven't seen him much since he's been back from the field."

"Not much? Try not at all." Deirdre put a marker in the book and placed it on the desk. "I hadn't told you yet, but I'm not staying for the next term."

Ann's face registered genuine surprise, but her intuition told her this was more than just a career adjustment.

"Is it Jack?"

Deirdre held her hands up in bewilderment. "Who knows? No, not entirely. I like to think that I wouldn't throw in the towel on a professional matter because of some schoolgirl crush." She stopped. "No, it's not a schoolgirl crush, Ann. I love him, but I don't see how we can have any future. I don't know why I ever did. Oh, and there's the small matter of his not being in love with me. That's always a little inconvenient in a prospective mate."

Ann tilted her head quizzically, her blue eyes both compassionate and slightly amused. "Now, Deirdre, he didn't say he wasn't in love with you, did he?"

"Well, not exactly. But he didn't say he was either!"

"Give the man a chance. Don't be so impatient or so pessimistic."

"Oh, Ann, I guess I'm just tired of waiting. And it's not just Jack. He was right when he said that a tactical signal unit wasn't suited to on-post classes. And frankly I don't like being at the beck and call of a CO, military maneuvers, and . . ."

"And you don't like digging latrines." However briefly, that allowed Deirdre to see the absurd side of her experience in Germany. She at least couldn't complain that it hadn't been an adventure—more adventure than she wanted, perhaps.

Ann walked over and put her hand on Deirdre's shoulder. "You gave it a good try—all of it. And who knows how things may yet turn out. For now, though, let's just have a good holiday. There will be time enough for all this later. Let's go. I'm starved. The cranberries await!"

Since it required more energy to refuse than

to accept, Deirdre reluctantly grabbed her heavy coat and gloves. The season had changed. How it had changed.

Later, as they stood in line, waiting their turn, Deirdre saw Jack come in from the opposite door. He wandered casually up and down the long cafeteria-style tables and benches, greeting and being greeted. He had seen her when he first came in, but after a long searching look, he had ignored her. Deirdre was so caught up in watching him that she didn't hear Ann and Lane's repeated question.

"Deirdre, did you hear? We wondered what you were doing for Christmas." Ann asked. Then she and Lane exchanged conspiring glances and smiles. "We have *other* plans, of course." Ann giggled.

Deirdre remembered that their wedding date was the seventeenth of December; they would be honeymooning at Christmas. As she was about to reply that she would be doing nothing except packing for home and feeling even more miserable than she did now, a PFC came into the mess hall and handed Jack a note. He took it casually and read it. His face went ashen. He reread it as if not believing its contents. He combed his fingers through his hair and let his hand rest on his eyes for a split second as if wanting to wipe away whatever message he had just seen. Then he said something to the PFC, who nodded grimly, and walked quickly from the hall without speaking to anyone else.

Ann and Lane had observed the scene too. They all looked at each other. Deirdre finally volunteered, "Maybe I'd better go see what the problem is."

"I'll go with you, if you want," Lane offered.

"No, you go ahead and eat. I wasn't hungry anyway."

She stepped outside; Jack must have almost run because he was nowhere to be seen. She wrapped the heavy green wool coat around her. It was one of the few items that she had bought "on the economy" in one of the upscale German department stores in Frankfurt. She was glad of its well-made quality on this bitterly cold day. No snow yet, but the lovely golden-hued autumn light and leaves had completely given way to a grey, bare landscape. As she walked quickly toward the company building, she noticed very few others out, and those few were heading in the direction of the mess hall.

The anteroom of HQ was almost eerie in its silence, yet there was the unmistakable feel of someone else present, a strong feeling of another human being—a sixth sense which must go back countless generations to when a human being might need that perception of a fellow being, either as warning or comfort. Deirdre wasn't sure how she felt at this particular moment, for she knew that it was Jack whose presence she was aware of.

"Hello," she called. "Anyone here?" No reply. Deirdre continued to walk through, slowly, step by step. Still no reply; now she was beginning to be concerned.

Finally, she was in the middle of the deserted outer office and could see through the partially opened door of Jack's office. She could see one of the lamps turned on, but no other light. She could also see the figure of Jack, elbows on his desk, his head in his hands. He was so still he could have been a statue.

Something was very wrong. More gently and softly, she called his name again. This time he very slowly raised his head, staring straight at the opposite wall, not at her. If he was in shock, she didn't want to add to the trauma by startling him into a response.

With relief, she saw him turn his head gradually to the doorway where she stood. He stared at her for a moment like someone whose mind was elsewhere. She had never seen such a look of total defenselessness on any human being. It both scared her and moved her profoundly.

"Deirdre?" His voice sounded low and gruff, not weak or faint as she had expected.

"Jack, it's me. What is it? What happened?"

He buried his head in his hands again, briefly, then looked up sharply, as if knowing he couldn't hide from his agony any longer. Deirdre saw now that he held a crumpled piece of paper in his hand, the same that had been handed too him in the mess hall. He held it up and it trembled in his hand like a small pathetic flag of surrender. "I just got this. From Oregon. My brother and his wife. They were going to Thanksgiving dinner at some friends' in the Gorge. An ice storm hit . . ." His voice faltered briefly as Deirdre realized what the awful news must be. He cleared this throat and continued. "Their car skidded into oncoming traffic. They were, were . . . killed instantly." Here his voice failed as if he had literally been drained of breath to speak words. Then Deirdre had a horrible thought.

"Molly? Not Molly too?"

Jack sat immobile for a moment; Deirdre thought she would burst before she heard the answer, but she also knew she couldn't, wouldn't rush him. *Oh, please, not Molly too,* she silently pleaded.

Then Jack shook his head. "No, thank heaven for small mercies. She was in the back, seat-belted in. She has a few bumps and bruises, but miraculously no serious injuries. They haven't told her . . . yet."

"Oh, Jack, I'm so, so sorry." She knew the words sounded so small, so inadequate, but she also knew from experience that the clichéd words and phrases brought whatever comfort and sympathy and love were behind them. She hoped Jack could feel that wellspring of emotion she now felt for him.

Whether he did or didn't, when he looked up at her, tears now streaming down his face, she knew she didn't have to say anything more. She walked over to him as he reached out for her and buried his head against her shoulder and sobbed, at last giving voice to wordless tears.

Chapter Ten

Two weeks later Deirdre was standing in the room in the barracks that was now hers alone. Ann had been officially discharged on December tenth and was now staying with the German pastor and his family until the wedding. If Deirdre thought that Ann glowed with happiness before, it was nothing to the radiance she took on once she had shed that "green machine": the fatigues, boots, and cap that tended to make one forget that the military was made up of individuals. Individuals who experienced love and joy—and loss and pain. Everything, every thought, brought her back to Jack. How she missed him.

She slipped on the fabric pumps that had been dyed a forest green. She stepped back and looked at her form in the long chipped mirror that hung on one wall of the room. The dress she and Ann had picked out was of the same green as the shoes, only in satin. It was a simple Empire gown with deep red rosettes worked around the neckline and short cap sleeves. Ann had chosen the colors, of course, because of the Christmas season, but both the style and the color complemented Deirdre's natural good looks. Her hair in particular was striking as it tumbled in rich black waves over her shoulders. And any shade of green enhanced her mercurial eyes.

She hoped that Jack would be back in time for the wedding the following week. Lane still wanted him to "stand up" for him. And it would be a chance to tell him good-bye for the last time.

The Army, of course, had granted "compassion leave" for him to attend his brother and sister-in-law's funeral. And to tend to little Molly. In the brief conversation they had before Jack left on Thanksgiving Day for the Frankfurt Airport, Deirdre had learned that Jack was Molly's legal guardian.

She wondered how he would handle being

a single dad in the military. Would he even stay in the military? Perhaps this tragedy would be the deciding factor. She felt an almost physical stab of pain as she thought of his future, simply because she no longer believed that she would be a part of it. She had already given her notice about going home after finals in another week. And after, of course, Ann and Lane's wedding.

A knock on the door interrupted her thoughts. "Yes?"

One of the new PFCs peeked her head around the corner. "Deirdre? Capt. Mackenzie is here to see you. He's downstairs, outside."

Deirdre hoped she didn't seem too eager as she practically fell out of her pumps trying to shake them off. "Thanks, Amy. I'll be right down."

She then glanced at her mirror, dabbed on a shade of russet lipstick that was flattering without being too obvious, and put a drop of perfume on her palms, rubbing furiously. The maid of honor dress! She didn't have to time to change. She simply slipped on a pair of old flats and ran downstairs, nodding a smile at Amy, and went out the door. For a moment she thought she would gasp out loud, but fortunately she caught herself in time.

The change in Jack in just two weeks had been astonishing. He must have lost ten pounds, and the normally healthy flush to his cheeks was chased away by a pale, sad-eyed look. Although she ached to realize how much he must have suffered in the past two weeks, she also felt more attracted to him, physically and emotionally, than she ever had. The ordeal of the last two weeks had weathered his robust handsomeness, but handsome—heart-tuggingly handsome—he remained.

He smiled as he saw her, but it was the smile of a man who still had a heart flooded with grief. It was a smile that bobbed like debris in a dark tide of emotion. "Deirdre." He said her name the way he had on their first date, softly, clearly like a magical chant.

"Jack." She went to him and hugged him briefly. "How are you doing?"

He shrugged in the old familiar way. "Okay, I guess." He looked at her again with some of his old sparkle. "You look beautiful. That for the wedding?" He nodded at the gown.

"Yes, how did you know?"

"The cat's out of the bag now. I talked to Lane this morning. I guess I'm going to be your opposite number at the wedding. Can we walk for a while? Will you be all right in that dress? The weather has turned rather mild for this time of year."

"Sure. It's nice today, but let me get a sweater."

"Don't bother. Here." He took off his corduroy jacket and placed it gently around her shoulders. "Come on."

They started ambling slowly down the short winding path of the barracks yard. They walked silently, Deirdre letting him take the lead. Soon they had reached the edge of the kaserne, and Jack motioned to the forest across the street. "Let's walk over there. The weather isn't threatening rain." They crossed the street, and began walking where they had first driven and parked several months earlier, and where they had walked and picnicked with Molly,

Jack was still silent. Finally Deirdre thought that some tactful questioning might make it easier for him to begin talking.

"How is Molly dealing with it?"

"As well as could be expected, I suppose. She was inconsolable at first, naturally." He shook his head. "That was the hardest thing I've ever had to do—or ever will. But it was one thing I could do for Pat and Ron. Or rather, the *first* thing I can do for them." He looked at Deirdre. "You know, don't you, that I'm Molly's guardian?"

She nodded. "You told me before you left, remember?"

He gently slapped his forehead. "Oh, that's right. I think I'm still in a bit of a fog."

"Of course, Jack. That's understandable. You've been through a tremendous shock. And you must have had a lot of details and arrangements to see to. Where is Molly?"

"She's staying with Pat and Ron's friends in the Gorge, the ones they were going to visit. They have a couple of kids Molly's age; she'll be fine there. For now."

Deirdre looked at Jack as he continued on, staring at the ground, seemingly lost in thought again. To bring him back she asked some inconsequential questions.

"Where is the 'Gorge'?"

"The Columbia River Gorge? It's northeast of Portland, on the edge of the Cascade Mountains. A glorious, ruggedly beautiful place. But it is notorious for sudden, brutal drops in temperature in winter. Blasts of arctic air from Canada can turn what was a damp but moderate day in Portland into a treacherous bout of ice and freezing rain in the Gorge. That's what happened to them; they were caught totally by surprise." He had seemed to be enlivened as he talked, but inevitably he seemed to come up against an inner wall of grief that knocked him into silence once again.

"Jack, what's going to happen to Molly?"

He glanced at her, then said edgily, "I told you. I'm her guardian. She's going to live with me."

Deirdre turned back in the direction of the kaserne. With a wave of her hand she asked, "There? On the kaserne?"

He didn't speak for a minute, then replied, "No."

"No?"

"You know as well as I do that I had already half made up my mind to leave the Army, ironically to go back to Oregon to help with the business so Ron could spend more time with his family. This, being Molly's guardian, makes it a hundred-percent certain that it's the right thing to do." He paused, looking at her with that searching way of his and said, "It's not quitting. It's just deciding that another commitment is more important than the one I've made to the Army the last the years or so."

Deirdre knew what he was referring to. "I don't think it's quitting either, Jack."

"I've decided to bring our—my—cousins into the business more, especially the traveling part. I'm going to stay put in Oregon. There's a little girl who is an orphan now. I'm her nearest relative." He stopped, choked with emotion. He cleared his throat. "I'm leaving for home again after the first of the year. Molly will be all right until then, and I have some paperwork and packing to do." Then he motioned to the clearing where they had had such a wonderful autumn picnic with Molly. It seemed so long ago now, but it was only a few months, only a season away.

"Well, I guess we'll both be leaving then. I did give my notice to the University. I'm going home the first week of January also. I have to finish up final grades and such, and I'll try to help the new instructor. I hear she's fresh out of grad school and very idealistic. Regular ball of fire." Jack caught her mild self-mockery and for the first time since the accident smiled. Deirdre went on. "I guess I *am* quitting, as you pointed out. You were right. About a lot of things."

"Well, it's probably the wise thing to do. To leave, I mean."

Deirdre was a little hurt by his lack of reaction, even though she no longer harbored any hope about their future together. She still wished that he had gotten a little angry or said "I told you so." At least that would have shown he cared.

"Well, I'm glad you agree," she huffed.

Abruptly, he stopped and turned. He placed his hands firmly but gently on her shoulders. "Deirdre, why don't we stop playing games, stop trying to pretend that we don't care so we don't get hurt. I love you. I have almost from the first time I saw you." He smiled. "Certainly from the first time I said your name. Deirdre. Remember? I said it as if it were magic. It was. It is."

Her heart pounding, she whispered, "I remember."

"Deirdre, you are idealistic, quick-tempered, obstinate, and sometimes too much on the defensive. You're also the most fascinating woman I've ever known, and I decided a long time ago, more or less"—he smiled—"that we were meant to be together. That sixth sense I told you about once . . . well, it's been telling me loud and clear for weeks that you're Miss Right, or Ms. Right, or Instructor Right, or whatever you want to be called."

Deirdre's eyes were shining with tears and her hands were trembling but she still managed to laugh. That secret window had flown open again. Forever this time.

Taking that as positive encouragement, Jack went on. "I can't help but think that somehow, some way, there is a reason for everything. No, I can't say that—there is no reason for Ron and Pat getting killed, none that I can know in this lifetime anyway. But I do think that as one destiny ends, another begins in its wake. Molly needs me now. I think that's my destiny. But I need you too, Deirdre. You're my destiny."

"A chuid de'n tsaoghal," she said softly.

"What, darlin'?" he murmured as he reached out to stroke her cheek.

" 'You're my share of the world.' It's the only Gaelic phrase my father ever taught me."

"It's beautiful. Deirdre, my share of the world," he repeated in an almost hushed voice. Then he pulled away from her and said, "We've got to do this right. This moment will pass into Mackenzie family legend." He got down on one knee, and took a small, worn burgundy velvet box from his pocket. The little box creaked as he snapped back the lid and removed a shimmering stone of deepest red encircled by tiny diamonds. "It's a garnet. It belonged to my grandmother." He took her hand, looking up at her with eyes that themselves were like jewels. With a firm voice he asked, "Will you marry me, Deirdre? Please? 'Come live with me and be my love'?"

Blushing, she laughed softly, answering, " 'And we will all the pleasures prove/That valleys, groves, hills, and fields,/Woods, or steepy mountain yields.' Yes, Jack. Yes, my share of the world."

He then slipped the ring on her finger; it was almost a perfect fit. "You'll get your forests after all, darling Deirdre. No castles or knights in shining armor, perhaps, but lots of trees and at least one little girl to teach everything you know about poems and poets, paragraphs and punctuation."

They were both laughing now, and he was holding her close. Deirdre quizzically raised an eyebrow. "At least one little girl?"

"I expect that we'll turn out a few charming high-spirited cousins for little Molly in due course."

"Will we now? By the way, I don't need a knight in shining armor. I already have the 'jack'—the Jack of Hearts. The one who grows up to live happily ever after, remember?"

"I remember, I remember." And then they spoke no more.

* * *

One sunny but chill morning the next week, Jack, Deirdre, and a few dozen others gathered in an old brown-brick church with black iron latticework on the doors and windows. They were there to witness the former Spec. Ann Shubert become Mrs. Lane Phillips.

Inside the small chapel, wood pews, polished naturally by two hundred years of worship, gleamed in the filtered light. It was a light that changed almost imperceptibly by the minute as the winter sun slid across the sky, peering through the stained glass at the ceremony below: shining red through a saint's robe or blue through Mary's or purple through the wine at Cana. Rose-scented candles and sprays of fresh flowers perfumed the air. The bride was lovely in ivory silk and lace, holding a bouquet of tiny red rosebuds and pink baby's-breath. The groom was handsome in his dress Class A uniform with its polished brass and medals. But Deirdre thought the best man was handsome beyond words, and he for his part thought that no maid of honor should look as radiantly, confidently beautiful as Deirdre.

In an atmosphere of simple, stately joy, the pastor spoke the final benediction on the newly married couple. As she listened to his words, Deirdre glanced down at the oval garnet on her hand and marveled at how this multifaceted gem, almost black in its intense red, reflected perfectly the whole spectrum of glowing color that bathed the sanctuary: splinters of green, blue, yellow, violet, constantly changing, constantly alive. It occurred to her that her future with Jack would be like this, life and color and warmth in every season.